It had to come up sooner or later. Clark sighed. He still hadn't come up with a graceful way to answer comments like that. "It's not a new story. Bad boy goes off to the big city to find new ways to be bad, hits bottom, comes home a changed man." Clark pinched the bridge of his nose, thinking that sounded arrogant. "Or hopes he comes home a changed man. I'm still ironing out the kinks, as you already know."

"I think I remember hearing something about an accident. Was that the bottom you hit?" Melba asked.

Calling that night an accident was like calling an earthquake a bump in the road. It wasn't the kind of thing Clark could share with just anyone, despite the warm look in Melba's eyes. She was dealing with her life tilting in a different direction, and he knew what that felt like. Maybe that was why he felt so drawn to her.

Books by Allie Pleiter

Love Inspired

My So-Called Love Life
The Perfect Blend
*Bluegrass Hero
*Bluegrass Courtship
*Bluegrass Blessings
*Bluegrass Christmas
Easter Promises
  *"Bluegrass Easter"
†*Falling for the Fireman*
†*The Fireman's Homecoming*

Love Inspired Historical

Masked by Moonlight
Mission of Hope
Yukon Wedding
Homefront Hero
Family Lessons

Love Inspired Single Title

Bad Heiress Day
Queen Esther &
  the Second Graders of Doom

*Kentucky Corners
†Gordon Falls

ALLIE PLEITER

Enthusiastic but slightly untidy mother of two, RITA®
Award finalist Allie Pleiter writes both fiction and
nonfiction. An avid knitter and unreformed choco-
holic, she spends her days writing books, drinking
coffee and finding new ways to avoid housework.
Allie grew up in Connecticut, holds a B.S. in speech
from Northwestern University and spent fifteen
years in the field of professional fund-raising. She
lives with her husband, children and a Havanese dog
named Bella in the suburbs of Chicago, Illinois.

The Fireman's Homecoming

Allie Pleiter

Recycling programs
for this product may
not exist in your area.

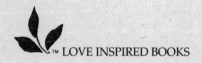

™ LOVE INSPIRED BOOKS

ISBN-13: 978-0-373-87819-2

THE FIREMAN'S HOMECOMING

www.LoveInspiredBooks.com

Printed in U.S.A.

And the God of all grace, who called you to his eternal glory in Christ, after you have suffered a little while, will himself restore you and make you strong, firm and steadfast.
—*1 Peter* 5:10

For the tireless, compassionate caregivers
serving their loved ones every day—
you are God's finest heroes of the heart.

Chapter One

Melba Wingate pushed the button on the hospital cafeteria vending machine again. *Please, Lord, I know this is Gordon Falls, but would it be too much to ask You to somehow send a grilled smoked gouda sandwich?* She peered without hope into the little mechanized windows rotating toward her. Sad, sanitary wedges of breaded ham and tuna salad stuttered into view. Those, and something labeled as—but barely resembling— turkey. It had been a long day, and her last meal had been two packages of cheese crackers from this machine six hours ago. She sighed and let her head fall against the cold hum of the machine window.

"No use looking for actual food in there."

Melba turned to see a man leaning against the hallway wall, one of the offending wedges in his hand with a single bite taken out of it. "I don't recommend the tuna. I'm not even sure I'd recommend the bread."

In dark pants and an official-looking white shirt, the man looked vaguely familiar. She felt as if she ought to know him by his red hair, but couldn't place the face. Just as she made out the name on his shirt badge, he extended a hand and said, "Clark Bradens." After a moment, he cocked his head to one side and said, "Aren't you…?" just as Melba said her name.

"Right." He nodded. "Mort's your dad. I heard you'd come back to town."

The familiar face and red hair made instant sense. She offered what she hoped was a grin and pointed to his name badge. "You were two years ahead of me in high school. George is your dad."

He took a final begrudging look at the sandwich and tossed it into a nearby garbage can. "I heard they brought Mort in here the other day. Everything okay?"

"Some bug hit him hard, but he'll be fine." She clutched her stomach, embarrassed at the loud growl it gave off. "I was trying to scare up some dinner, but I don't think I have too many edible options beside a Snickers bar here."

"You remember Dellio's just down the street? Not too many problems in this world can't be improved with their good cheeseburgers, and it'd be a quick trip."

Dellio's had been a favorite of hers in high school, and while she didn't do cheeseburgers anymore, their fries could still taunt her from half a mile away. Melba salivated. "I don't eat meat. Anymore, I mean. And I can't really leave Dad."

He paused for a moment, then checked his watch. "I've got twenty minutes. They make a mean grilled portobello for you veggie types. I could have it and fries back here in fifteen for you if you want."

Melba blinked. The Clark Bradens she remembered was not the kind of guy who played fetch out of sympathy. Then again, the Clark Bradens she remembered would have been the last man she'd have expected to put on a uniform for the Gordon Falls Volunteer Fire Department—especially with his dad as chief. The margins of far too many high school notebooks were filled with odes to Clark's wavy red hair and dreamy green eyes, but attributes like "responsible" or "civic-minded" never seemed to come up. He'd been the kind of bad-boy motorcycle rebel that mothers warned daughters about, known for luring cheerleaders to their doom.

The man before her didn't look anything like that. Oh, the handsome hadn't left, but the dark edge was long gone. Or maybe she was just tired. His smile was almost sweet, bearing a touch of the weariness she felt down to her bones this evening. Who cared about moral fiber when the man was offering Dellio's fries? Life had handed her too many reasons to crave them today. "I'm in." She dug into her wallet.

Clark pushed her wallet back down toward the handbag. "I'll spring. They give us a firefighter's discount anyway. Give me your dad's room number and I'll bring it up."

"Really?"

"Think of me as the Gordon Falls Welcome Wagon." He nodded to the machine of questionable sustenance behind her. "Or just a guy who's eaten too many of those."

Melba was too hungry to refuse. "Room 614. You just became my hero."

"Shh…" Clark gave her the wink he was known for back in the day. "Don't let that kind of thing get out."

Melba heard her father's agitated voice as she got off the sixth floor elevator.

"Calm down, Mr. Wingate, she'll be back in a moment."

"Where is she? Where'd she go?" The angry, confused panic in her father's voice was a knife to her chest. She clutched her handbag to her side and took the hallway at a jog, only barely catching the resigned look from the station nurse as she turned the corner.

"We need to tell Melba."

Dad had been doing so well this afternoon. She tossed her bag onto the vinyl chair and grabbed her father's hand. "Hey, I'm right here, Dad."

"Don't leave like that, Maria. Don't do that." The knife buried in her ribs twisted harder when he called her by her mother's name.

"He was fine until a minute ago, really," the nurse said.

Melba nodded, shifting to place herself in her dad's line of vision. "I'm here. I just left for a second but I'm back now."

Her father's eyes found her, the trembling grip on her hand tightening. "Maria."

Melba swallowed. It seemed so cruel to correct him when he got like this. "It's okay," Melba whispered to the nurse. "I think he'll settle down now."

She felt the nurse's hand on her back. "He is better than he was yesterday, remember that." They'd done this more than a few times since Mort had been admitted with fevers two days ago. "I'll come back with the evening sedative in about an hour."

The nurse left and Melba sank onto the bed's edge, weary. She stroked her father's right hand, hating the blue-black bruises. They'd moved the IV needle to his left hand yesterday when he'd pulled it out of his right hand.

"I'm sick." His voice took on a frail, childish quality that opened a black hole in Melba's stomach.

"Well, yes, you caught some kind of bug, but the fever's almost gone so you'll go home soon."

"It's wrong, Maria."

"Nothing's wrong, Dad. You *should* go to the hospital when you're sick. It'll be fine by tomorrow, you'll see."

"Maria, I'm telling you, it's wrong. She needs to know."

She dismissed the useless reply of "But I'm Melba, Dad," and kept stroking his hand instead. "Tell her what?"

Dad grew agitated, his mouth working for the words. He seemed to lose words so much more now, and that seemed so cruel—he was still two years shy of sixty. "I hate that she's not mine." He moaned it, as if the words broke his heart in half. Melba froze, the strength of his regret grabbing at her, forcing her attention as much as the clutching grip he had on her hand. "She ought to know she's not mine. It's wrong. It has to be fixed. We need to tell her, Maria." Anger narrowed his eyes and he shook Melba's arm with every word.

Melba's blood ran as cold as her father's hand. *Not mine?* What did that mean? He couldn't possibly be saying what she thought, could he? The knot of worry in her stomach hardened to a dark ball of suspicion, but she tried to push it away. Such a thing wasn't possible. Dad wasn't himself. She shook it off, just as she'd shaken off the irrational fear that he'd somehow not survive a simple bout of the stomach flu. The man in front of her was Dad. Weak, confused, but Dad all the same.

"Keeping it from her was a mistake." The bark of command came back to his voice, iron-strong out of a man who had looked yesterday as though he were made of paper. "Why can't you see that?" He rattled her hand for emphasis. "Where's Melba? Find her. I'll tell her myself if you won't."

The dark suspicious knot began to pull tighter. This was not one of Dad's "wanderings," the wishful conversations Mort invented with Melba's mom, gone two years now. He'd gotten angry before, but it was always a generalized, frustrated anger, never clear and pointed like this. This had another tone altogether. It seemed almost like he was remembering a real problem he and her mother had struggled with—an argument they had actually had. But the things he was saying didn't make any sense. She had no idea what to do with his strange actions or his words.

"I'm here, Dad, I'm right here." Melba peeled the clenched gray hand off hers and stroked it until the fist softened. She needed this strange tormented man to go away, needed Dad to come back and tell her that nothing was amiss. "I'm your daughter. I'm Melba. I'm right here."

Her voice saying her own name seemed to pull him from the fog. Dad's narrowed eyes softened in affection and recognition. His whole countenance changed as if the last thirty seconds had happened to someone else. As relieved as she was to see the change, it disturbed her, too. She'd done loads of research, trusted Dad's doctors, and had three friends whose parents were living with the same disease. She'd thought she was prepared. Still, the split-second change of his emotions always pummeled her. Alzheimer's was like an invitation into a house of mirrors, never knowing which face belonged to the Dad who loved her and which belonged to the fast-aging man who didn't recognize her. There had been days lately where it seemed he lost his bearings midsentence.

"Where's your mother, Melba?" His kindness and clarity startled her—where had it been a moment ago? Why now and not the dozen other times she'd told him who she was? "I need to talk to your mother."

He'd become reconnected and yet still not quite back to reality. The emotional whiplash rattled her again, compounded by what she'd just heard. Or thought she heard. Or shouldn't hear. She wanted to throw her hands up in panicked frustration, but kept still. Who knew what she'd just heard or if it meant anything at all? "Mom's been gone two years, Dad, remember?" She tried to keep her voice soft and reassuring, despite her thundering pulse. She made herself ask, "What did you need to tell her?"

Dad's brows furrowed in sad confusion. "I forget. I forget she's gone, you know?" He seemed like a wayward child seeking forgiveness, aware he'd done something wrong but unable to say what. Somehow the disease had taken a giant leap forward during these three days, scaring him as much as it scared her.

Dad's attention wandered off. She watched his thumb absentmindedly rub the ring finger on his left hand, searching for the wedding band the hospital had asked her to remove along with his watch when he was admitted. The ring had still been warm from his hand when she'd slipped it on her thumb for safekeeping and she'd kept it on since. Did he even recognize it was missing? Did he even notice its odd home on her right hand as she touched him? "I know, Dad." Melba fought back the lump in her throat—and the roiling in her stomach—to force brightness into her voice. "Hey, it's just us pals now, remember?"

The phrase never failed to bring a broad smile. "Just us pals now." He looked around the room as if he'd just entered instead of been here three days. "Let's go home. I don't need all this junk."

"All this junk" was Dad's catch-all term for everything medical, and he had lots of "junk" these days. Too much. She'd spent nearly a year ignoring the red flags of warning that began a while after Mom died; the missed date here or the lost word there. A few months ago those flags refused to be ignored as it became clear Dad wasn't just pushing sixty, he was sick. Getting sicker. Packing up her Chicago life to move back home felt like diving into a bottomless black pit, but she'd known it was the right thing to do. More than just "honor thy father," she loved him, shared his loneliness now that Mom was home in Heaven. Sure, it was difficult—and so painfully early for a man as vibrant as her father—but Melba never doubted the choice. She was exactly where she was supposed to be. From now on, it was going to get harder. Somewhere in the back of her mind she knew she'd think of this day as "the day it started getting worse." Her stomach rolled and she felt ill instead of hungry.

"Doc Nichols says you *do* need all this junk. At least for a bit. That flu hit you pretty hard, and he wants you stronger before he lets you go home."

"I'm fine."

Melba raised her eyebrows and pointed to the IV line. "Oh, really?"

"I'll be fine once they unplug me from this getup."

Melba fiddled with the plastic pitcher of ice water on the bedside tray. Her anxious curiosity about his outburst was like an undertow, pulling her off her feet no matter how she scrambled for shore. Against every instinct, knowing it would be fruitless, she still couldn't stop from asking, "So, what did you want to talk to Mom about?"

"Did I ask for… Hey, why are you wearing my ring? On your *thumb?* Give that back, it looks ridiculous on you like that." He reached for her hand only to wince when the tension on the IV line tugged at the needle in his hand. He scowled, a seven-year-old's tantrum brewing under the wrinkles of his fifty-eight years.

Melba poked her thumb into the air. "I kind of like it. All the cool kids are wearing rings on their thumbs now."

"You're twenty-six, not a cool kid, and I want that back."

How could he do that? Remember her age with stunning clarity and then forget his wife of nearly thirty years had died? He'd phoned Melba a month ago—at work no less—and asked her calmly what she wanted for her sixteenth birthday. The day-to-day randomness of his disease hurt almost more than the ultimate decline it heralded. "You eat all that delightful turkey dinner on that plate so Doc Nichols signs off on your release, and I'll hand it to you personally."

Dad picked up a fork and poked at the beige slab in questionable gravy. "Do they think I've already forgotten what real food tastes like?"

Melba hated when he made those kind of comments—the ones that hinted he knew how far he'd slipped and how fast. Alzheimer's at this age was bad enough, but to be aware of your own decline seemed too cruel for anyone. She wanted to run into the bathroom and sob but she plastered a smile on her face. "Think of it as incentive. Choke down the bad food so you can go home to Barney's good cooking."

Dad smiled at the mention of the hefty woman who came every afternoon to tend house and fix him dinner. Barbara Barnes, or "Barney," as everyone called her, had insisted on coming by daily even after Melba moved in. "Barney's meatloaf," he sighed, resigning himself to the penance of hospital turkey.

She gestured like a game-show hostess. "And it could be yours if you just behave for one more day."

"I'll share." He hoisted the fork in her direction.

Melba held up a hand. "No, thanks. I've got someone bringing me Dellio's in a few minutes. I may even let you have a fry if you polish off your turkey." It sounded so horridly parental, the unnatural role reversal of eldercare lamented by every book and friend.

"Well, isn't that dandy, you getting one of those cheeseburgers you like so much and leaving me with these mushy peas."

Melba sighed. She'd been a vegetarian for six years.

Clark checked his watch and winced. "You know, Plug, I need to ban the phrase 'I'll be right back' from my vocabulary."

The firehouse dog offered a sympathetic woof that sounded far too much like "I told you so" before wandering off to the kitchen.

Clark followed. "Hey, Pop? Do you know when visiting hours are over at the hospital?"

"Eight," came his father's voice over the usual mealtime chatter from the firehouse dining room.

It was seven-fifteen. An hour after he'd promised Melba Wingate he'd be "back in fifteen" with a meal from Dellio's. Clark glowered at the pager fixed to his belt. "What? Do you have some kind of radar to know when it's the worst time to go off?" Some days that little black device felt more like a ball and chain than life-saving technology—especially when it signaled a false alarm like it had this evening. If he ever got his hands on the kid who pulled that fire alarm over at the high school, it wouldn't be pretty. "Do you know if you can hear the siren over at the hospital?" It was a slim chance Melba heard the siren and realized he'd been called into duty, but it was better than her thinking him a jerk.

Pop poked his head up from the pot he was stirring. He rarely went out on calls anymore, so he was in a red apron and holding a bowl of chili—it had become his role to ensure everyone got fed once they came in off a call. "I expect not. Folks need to get their sleep over there, you know. You want cheese on yours?"

Clark grabbed his keys off a hook in the hallway. "I'll pass. I was supposed to be somewhere an hour ago."

"You need to eat and they'll understand."

Clark shrugged his shoulders. "I'm not so sure."

Pop sat back on one hip. "Who's not going to understand a volunteer firefighter going out on call?" It was more of an accusation than a question. Chief George Bradens brooked no disrespect whatsoever where the Gordon Falls Volunteer Fire Department was concerned. Besides, Clark had made plans to have dinner with his dad even before the call. Before Melba.

"I met Melba Wingate over at the hospital. Mort's daughter. She looked in a bad way, so I told her I'd run and get her something from Dellio's and bring it back to her so she wouldn't have to leave her dad."

Some kind of weird shadow passed over Pop's face. "She'll get over it. She just hasn't lived here long enough to remember what it is we all do around here."

"Maybe, but I feel bad."

"Well, you ought to."

"Even if I stop by Dellio's first, there would still be a half an hour of visiting hours by the time I could get to the hospital. I'll try a last-ditch effort in case she's still there. You'll still be here when I get back, right?" he called as he ducked out the door. After two seconds he circled back to add "Mort's doing fine," but not before he realized Pop hadn't asked after Mort.

Which was odd because Pop asked after everyone. Pop was like Gordon Falls's universal grandfather, poking his nose into everyone's welfare. He'd always thought there was something odd about the chill between those two, but then again he'd just stood Pop up for dinner. Again. So much for trying to prove to his father that he'd put his old, irresponsible ways behind him. Why was it he had such a gift for disappointing people? He put it from his mind as he thumbed through his cell phone to the listing for Dellio's "call ahead and pick up" line.

Chapter Two

Clark knocked on the hospital room door even though it was partway open. "Better late than never, I hope."

The pile of snack wrappers on the side table by Melba made him wince. She looked worse than earlier, looking over her shoulder at him with weary eyes. Her father seemed to be dozing, his head turned toward the window and a blanket tucked up over his thin shoulders. He didn't know Mort all that well, but it didn't take a lot of familiarity to see the man was in bad shape. His thin, wiry body slumped without energy against the hospital bed.

"That was a long fifteen minutes." Her words were lifeless, as if she were too tired to be angry.

Clark palmed the pager at his side. "Got a call. Normally I take cell numbers because this kind of thing happens all the time, but I didn't have yours. Sorry I kept you waiting."

She pushed a strand of hair out of her face. She wore exotic, artsy jewelry on several fingers—the handmade kind with lots of colored stones—and a bulky gold band on one thumb. "It's okay." He looked past the dark brown curls to see red-rimmed eyes. She'd been crying.

"No, it's not." He kept his voice soft as he walked farther into the room. "Hey, look, are you going to be okay? No offense, but you look like you need a lot more help than just a decent meal."

She took a deep breath and swept up the pile of wrappers into the trash can. "It's been…a bit rough today, that's all. Harder than I thought."

Even though his training as a first responder injected him into people's moments of pain all the time, he felt this intrusion keenly. "What isn't?" He placed the bag on the table, uncomfortable but still unwilling to leave. "Is he in pain?"

"Just really confused. He wakes up not remembering where he is or why he's here."

"Sounds understandable." Her watched her pull herself wearily out of the chair. "You think he'll be better once he gets back home?"

It was the wrong question. "I'm sure he will." Disbelief pushed a false brightness into her words even as fear leapt up in her eyes. "Thanks, I'm starved."

"I'm glad I made it under the wire. Another ten minutes and they wouldn't have let me in. I'd have been forced to eat that giant fungus for you."

She managed a small smile that broadened when she opened the bag of French fries and the savory aroma filled the room. The half-eaten contents of the bag sitting on the seat of Clark's car held testament to the truth that nothing in the world grew an appetite faster than the scent of Dellio's fries.

The aroma even roused Mort, who groaned and rolled his head on the pillow to face them. His ashen face startled Clark. It seemed impossible that the man in that bed was nearly the same age as his own robust father—they looked decades apart.

Mort's brows furrowed in confusion, staring at Clark as if he were a misplaced object. Melba walked over to touch her father's arm, her whole body reacting to his wakefulness. Something dark and hard flashed in Mort's eyes, and he began to pull himself up off the bed. "What's *he* doing here?" he snapped.

"That's Clark Bradens, Dad. He brought…"

"How dare he come here?" Mort jabbed an accusatory finger in Clark's direction. "You swore to me, Maria, you said you'd never…"

"Dad, it's Melba. Calm down, okay?" With a flash of a look in Clark's direction, Melba pushed her father back onto the bed and hit the nurse call button.

"Get him out of my home!" Mort yelled, and Clark backed up toward the door.

"I'm sorry, he's not himself." Melba struggled to keep Mort from rising.

Clark felt awful for not being able to help, but it seemed clear that moving any closer to Mort would just escalate things. "I'll just go." The nurse came in behind him as he ducked out of the room.

"Go away and don't come back!" Mort's brittle voice called behind him.

Her father's angry words still echoed in Melba's head as she stared into her tea the next morning. The chill of them made her pull the afghan Mom had knitted for her first apartment tighter around her shoulders. Its blue-and-green design didn't fit this house's color scheme, but then again nothing from her Chicago apartment looked at home in this country bungalow. She was at home and out of place at the same time.

The color clash was a mirror of her mood. Events felt confusing since last night, facts wouldn't fit together in neat patterns, and life itself felt disjointed and tangled.

"I'm..." she searched for the right verb as she stroked Pinocchio, the fat tabby who'd been their pet since Melba was sixteen "...tumbling into a new life today, hm?" *Tumbling* seemed like the best word. *Tumbling* was something set in motion not by her, but by things beyond her ability to control. *Tumbling* didn't imply control or direction—and she felt like none of those were in her grasp today. Pinocchio merely purred and pushed against her hand, the universal cat gesture for "more, please."

"Dad's coming home today. You'll get plenty of petting soon." Pinocchio was one of the few things guaranteed to calm Dad down when he got confused. Pinocchio and music. Melba had loaded Dad's favorite record album—a collection of old hymns played on the piano—onto her digital music player so she could play them for him in the hospital. She had it playing now. It was nice to have the music cue the long-remembered lyrics in her head—"Great is Thy Faithfulness" was a good message for someone thrashing their way through a huge life shift.

When she heard the cuckoo clock downstairs in the living room announce 8:00 a.m., Melba shook off the afghan and hoisted Pinocchio from her lap. Resolutely, she walked downstairs. *Face the day head-on, Melba girl.* Bright April sunshine filled the kitchen from the window over the sink. Melba let the light soak in, a welcome counterbalance to the cloudy way her soul felt today. Cued by the music, Melba sang the hymn's reassuring words as she loaded her breakfast dishes into the twenty-year-old dishwasher and spun the funky little dial to hear it gurgle to life.

Am I gurgling to life? Or about to drown?

Barney was sitting at the kitchen table making a shopping list when Melba came back downstairs dressed and showered. With a lopsided grin, she nodded toward the dishwasher. "You paid for that, didn't you?"

Melba had to laugh. "I'm used to living in an apartment building where you can run the dishwasher and the shower at the same time." She mimed a shiver. "Brrr, but at least I'm wide awake now. I don't suppose they have decent chai tea at the supermarket here, do they? I need better caffeine these days."

Barney laughed. She was a hefty, jolly woman, the kind whose eyes sparkled and whole body jiggled when she laughed. "Lipton's about as exotic as they get down at Morgan's Finer Foods, darlin'."

Melba added *Stop at Karl's Koffee and get some decent tea* to her mental list of "Dad Coming Home Tasks."

"Coming-home day," Barney said as she opened the door and surveyed the empty fridge. "Glad of it, too. I don't like to think of your dad holed up in one of those cold, harsh hospital rooms. He needs his things around him, you know?"

"He does, I know." Half of her was glad Dad was going to be discharged today, but the other half of her was anxious, even with Barney's offer of extra help. "Dr. Nichols just called the fever 'a bump in the road,' but I'm worried. He seemed to…" she searched again for the right verb "…unravel in a way he hasn't before."

It seemed a better way to put it than "I think he blurted out a deep dark secret about me," which was what the back of her mind had been yelling at her all morning despite every effort to ignore it.

"Hey," she called over her shoulder as she stuffed papers into a purple batik tote bag, "did Dad ever blurt stuff out at you…say things you're not sure he meant?" It didn't come off as casually as she tried to make it sound.

She felt Barney's hand on her shoulder and almost resisted turning, afraid she'd be unable to stop herself from crumpling into a tearful heap on the big woman's shoulders. "It's not him talking, child, it's the disease. Don't you dare take it personal when he gets mean like that."

Melba swallowed, unsure whether to be glad Barney half mistook her real question. "I know."

Barney pointed at her. "Do you *know* how glad— how well and truly glad—he was to know you were coming home to him? How much that meant to him? *Means* to him?"

"It means as much to me. He acts like it was this big sacrifice on my part, as if he has to make it up to me every waking moment, but I chose to come back. I would never have chosen not to come." She blinked back the tears that threatened. Over the last two days it felt like she'd spent more time swallowing back a sob than she spent breathing. She tugged what proved to be the last tissue from the box on the kitchen table.

Barney smirked and grabbed the grocery list from the table to add "tissues x 3" to her list. "There's too many youngsters would have chosen not to come, you know. Kids who bolt when life gets hard or messy. Life *is* hard and messy, I tell my Jake all the time." She cupped Melba's cheek like a doting grandmother. "The wise among us know you live into the hard, live into the mess, because running from it never works. It always comes and finds you." Barney waved her hands as if shooing her words like flies. "As if you need any such sermon on a day like today. How about I make sure there's a chocolate cake waiting for you and Mort when you get home? Jake'll tell you there's no healing power like that of a wise mama's chocolate cake."

Melba started to decline, and then decided a wise mama bearing chocolate cake was no gift horse to look in the mouth. Not today. "Just get some *skim* milk to go with it?"

Barney scowled a bit, obviously thinking anything "reduced fat" was an abomination of nature. The woman put whipping cream in her coffee, and was probably the reason Dad managed to keep most of his weight on when so many other of Dr. Nichols's patients dropped pounds. "And yogurt, if you don't mind," Melba added, remembering the full bag of fries she'd put away with glee last night. "Anything with 'light' on the label will do." She needed to get running again or her waistline would soon succumb to the ravages of the Barney Meal Plan.

"Call my cell when you know what time you'll be coming home. I'll make sure Jake swings by in case we need some of my son's manpower to get your dad up the steps."

Dad unable to get himself up his own front steps. The thought struck a cold note under her ribs. She grabbed the keys to her Prius and applied a smile to her face. "It'll be okay, Barney, I'm sure it will."

"Well, you know what they say."

Melba stopped with the door half-open. "What do they say?"

"It'll all be okay in the end. And if it ain't okay yet, well, then it ain't the end yet either."

Oh, no, Melba thought, *it's just the beginning.*

Clark caught sight of Melba as she walked down Tyler Avenue, Gordon Falls's main street, toward the corner that housed Karl's Koffee. He was glad she looked a bit stronger. He rushed across the street to tap her shoulder. "Hey, Melba, hi. Look, I'm really sorry about last night."

"You shouldn't apologize—you didn't do anything other than bring me dinner. I'm sorry Dad hauled off at you like that. I think maybe he thought you were someone else."

"I knew it wasn't about me. But being an hour late with your food? That was all me."

"Yeah, but you already apologized for that."

There was still so much weariness in her eyes. "That's some tough going with your dad. Is he coming home anytime soon?"

"I'm heading over there in a bit. Yesterday afternoon Dr. Nichols said he would probably come home today, but…" She shrugged while he pulled open the door to Karl's for her. "It's so up-and-down, you know?"

No, he didn't know. Pop was still as sharp as a tack and going strong at fifty-four, and while Mom's diabetes had taken her life too soon, it had never been the sort of drawn-out trauma Melba had ahead of her. "That memory-loss stuff seems so hard to handle."

"Most times it's not so bad but you…well…" She

blinked, and took a deep breath. "You caught him at his worst."

Clark felt an unwanted tug toward Melba and the huge burden she carried. He was always a softie for a damsel in distress, only now was absolutely not the time. Now was supposed to be all about his new job at the department, about making things right with Pop. Still, every lecture he'd given himself about professional focus couldn't stop the invitation from coming out of his mouth. "Buy you a cup of coffee?"

She looked up at him as if the thought of someone doing something nice for her were a foreign custom. "You don't owe me."

"I know." Now it was he who shrugged. "But if you were heading for Karl's I'm guessing you could use one."

She gave him a slip of a smile, just enough of a hint to let him know her full-blown grin would have distracted him for hours. *Cut that out, Bradens. You promised no female distractions. You get sidetracked and stupid when a woman enters the picture, and too much is on the line here.* She ordered a scone and some odd chai thing—soy milk and other strange ingredients—and surprised him by asking for a china mug instead of a to-go cup which made him feel obligated to do the same. It felt like cheating on his "no female distractions" policy when he slipped into the booth by the window—she obviously thought he'd meant a visit when he offered to buy her a drink, not just the purchase of a beverage. And it'd be rude to refuse, right? Sitting down for coffee. A friendly cup of coffee. Between friends. When was the last time he'd done that?

He didn't even know Karl's would serve in actual mugs, and he lived here.

And now, so did she. *Distractions*...

"Extra time." She sighed, looking around the folksy little coffeehouse. "I'd forgotten it existed. I'd also forgotten it only takes two seconds to get anywhere in Gordon Falls. I'm so used to leaving time for traffic."

"We don't really get Chicago-brand traffic in Gordon Falls. You can count the streetlights on one hand. Ah, but come some of the holiday weekends, just watch how the locals grumble that you can't park within a block of Tyler Avenue."

She gave a small laugh as she wrapped her hands around the large blue stoneware mug. She wore a dark purple nail polish and all those rings he'd noticed the other night. He couldn't tell if the exotic spicy scent that wafted toward him was from her hair or the tea, but its uniqueness intrigued him. And *that hair,* that mass of dark curls tumbling around her shoulders—how had he not remembered Melba Wingate and that hair? "You were a freshman when I was a junior, weren't you?" Clark had absolutely no remembrance of the teenage Melba. Sure, he knew her name—Wingate's Log Cabin Resort had been a Gordon Falls staple for years before they'd finally closed up shop after Mrs. Wingate died—but nothing else about her. "What did you do after school?"

Melba sipped her tea. "I went to design school in Chicago, and then got a job at a textile import house. I figured import-export was the perfect way to see the world. I got to do a few trips and was getting ready to go on a large-scale overseas buying expedition when things got..." Her eyes flashed up at him, then back into the mug. "…complicated. Work's been really nice about the whole thing, shifting me to handle their on-line catalogue while I'm here dealing with…Dad." She used a knife to cut her scone in half. A perfect, thought-ful cut. Artistic. "You?"

Clark thumbed the name badge on his shirt pocket. "Two years of criminal justice at the local commu-nity college, but I was never the kind of guy to finish things, so I went into firefighting pretty much after that. I worked in Detroit for seven years until I came back here."

"The big-city fireman."

"Well, Detroit. Maybe not as big as Chicago, but it makes up for it in intensity."

She sized him up as she ate a bite of her scone. "I never pegged you for the kind to come back home."

It had to come up sooner or later. Clark sighed. He still hadn't come up with a graceful way to answer com-ments like that. "It's not a new story. Bad boy goes off to the big city to find new ways to be bad, hits bottom, comes home a changed man." Clark pinched the bridge of his nose, thinking that sounded arrogant. "Or hopes he comes home a changed man. I'm still ironing out the kinks, as you already know."

She leaned back in the booth, finger running around the rim of her mug. "I think I remember hearing some-thing about an accident. Was that the bottom you hit?"

Calling that night an accident was like calling an earthquake a bump in the road. Talking about that point in his life was a four-hour conversation, not something for a quick morning coffee. It wasn't the kind of thing Clark could share with just anyone, despite the warm look in Melba's eyes. She was dealing with her life tilting in a different direction, and he knew what that felt like. Maybe that was why he felt so drawn to her. But she had enough trouble on her plate. Digging into his own mess with Melba Wingate was not on today's menu—on this year's menu—of good ideas. He drank down the last of his coffee and made a show of checking his watch—the only way he could think of to slip out of the oncoming conversation. "Yeah, well, that's a story needing way more time than you or I have."

She peered at her half-empty mug and scone with only a bite taken out of it. "I should probably head on over to the hospital." Her words lacked any sense of hurry whatsoever.

Clark's gut grew a black hole, and it wasn't from gulping his coffee. He was leaving her hanging—again—and he knew it, but he also knew that the potency of that topic with this woman was a bad combination. He could not get so personal with her and keep it "friendly." The goal here was to keep his focus on becoming the department's new chief, and Clark's terrible track record bore witness that any romantic entanglements would mess up the chance he had here in Gordon Falls. "No, stay, enjoy the sunshine. I just have to go… Appointment… Firehouse stuff." He wanted to whack his forehead for how lame that excuse sounded. "Hope things go well for your dad."

Her smile was polite but hollow. "Me, too. It's been a rough couple of days."

Clark made himself sit still a moment longer. "This is a good town, you know. People know your dad. They'll want to help, so don't be afraid to ask for it when you need it, okay? Barney knows everyone and Pastor Allen can have twelve casseroles at your house in under an hour—our deacons' board is like a SWAT team."

He was glad that got a laugh from her. He wanted her to get connected—it was just better if it wasn't to him. "I've been meaning to get settled in a church here."

With her words, a memory of high school Melba invaded his brain. A gawky, frizzy-haired teen girl heading up to the youth Bible study he used to make such fun of with his wild friends. How the world had changed for them both.

Chapter Three

"Okay, now, you're settled." Melba tucked the knitted afghan over Dad's knees. He looked so old, the recliner's worn cushions nearly swallowing his thin body.

"What a lot of work getting up those front steps." She couldn't tell if Dad's remark was in annoyance or admission. Did he have any sense of how frail he'd become? "When did we paint them that awful green?" He glared out the window at them, eyes narrowed in the expression of a man gloating over a vanquished foe.

She could almost laugh. Maybe it was better if Dad blamed the steps. "Two years ago. And the green's not so bad."

"It's all wrong. I liked them better when they were brown."

The most amazing details from way back would pop into his mind like that. The steps hadn't been brown for almost ten years—they'd been beige before they were green. Melba took her father's coat and hung it on the bentwood coatrack by the door. "Maybe we'll paint them this summer."

"I'd like that." The smile seemed to transform her

father's face, to roll back the years as it lit up his eyes. "I'm hungry. The food in there was lousy."

"Nutrition is boring," Barney declared, waltzing into the room with two sizable slices of chocolate cake. "So I'm banning healthy meals for the rest of the day." She winked at Dad as she put the fork into his right hand. For a while they'd thought he'd lost his appetite, getting surly at meals, until one supper he let it slip that he couldn't remember which hand to use. Now Barney slid the fork into his hand as if it were the most natural thing in the world. Barney was amazing at helping Dad without making him feel "helped." Melba had run out of ways to thank her.

"Where's your slice?"

Barney rubbed her hefty stomach. "Already gone. Someone had to make sure it was up to snuff."

"You're a doll," Dad said behind a mouthful of cake. "Delicious as always."

Picking up her handbag, Barney tapped Melba's shoulder. "I'll be at church for the women's committee till four. I'll be back to check on you and put the casserole into the oven at five so you all can eat at six. You all call me if you need anything. Anything at all."

"We've got cake, we'll be fine as can be," Dad said.

Barney smiled, but caught Melba's eyes with a silent "You going to be all right on your own?" raise of one eyebrow.

"Fine as can be," Melba echoed, banning all sounds of worry from her voice. In truth, she was more than a little nervous, wondering if Dad's fits of anger or anxiety would soon loom larger than she could handle. Looking back at him now, she saw just a happy old man eating cake in his favorite chair.

* * *

They passed the afternoon without incident, Dad napping while Melba formatted half a dozen digital catalogue pages for work and plowed through the pile of emails left unattended during the hospital stay. "I'll need to learn to give myself wider margins on deadlines," she wrote her boss, Betsy, in the email that submitted the catalogue pages, thankful that she'd had the cable company install wireless internet a week ago. "Life can get upended on a moment's notice over here." It annoyed her that the pages were a day behind schedule—usually Melba managed to get things in early. "On time is late for Melba," Betsy used to joke. She doubted anyone would say that anymore.

"Melba?" Dad's voice startled her, it was so clear and strong.

"Right here, Dad."

"It's four-thirty, isn't it?"

She glanced at the clock above the kitchen table where she'd been working. "Four twenty-eight, to be exact."

"Aren't I supposed to take one of those enormous pills now?"

Melba pulled the huge, multi-compartmented pill sorter toward her—recently refilled with some new additions—and consulted the list. "Wow, Dad, you're good. Yep, it's one of those big yellow ones." She filled a glass with water and brought him the pill with two others in the "Afternoon" compartment.

Dad made a face. "These are monsters. They used to be small and white."

They did. His memory was still there, peeking out,

holding on. "Well, Doc says you need a double dose for the next few weeks."

"Let *him* choke 'em down, then." He slid the collection into his mouth, grimaced, then swallowed. "I might need more cake to ease the way." Dad grinned up at her like a mischievous child.

"You'll spoil your supper."

"Fine by me."

He seemed so here, so alert and happy. "How about a cup of tea instead?" Some huge part of her wanted to sit with him right now and make him tell her all of whatever he'd begun to say back there in the hospital. Another part of her wanted to run, to put her fingers in her ears like a disobedient child, and pretend she'd never heard a thing. Mostly, she craved the connected gaze of his eyes, the true conversation he seemed capable of right now. The urge to hoard his salient moments, to stockpile his wisdom and affection, surged up until she bent over the recliner and gathered him in a fierce hug.

"What's this fuss?" His words spoke surprise but his eyes told her he knew what was behind her embrace.

"I'm just glad you're home," she managed, blinking too fast.

"You and me both, Melbadoll."

She laughed. "I think it's been fifteen years since you've called me that."

"You told me you hated it back in high school."

"What did I know back in high school?"

He laughed. It sputtered into a small cough, but it was a laugh just the same. Melba jumped on the tiny boost of courage it gave her. "Hey, Dad, guess who I ran into this morning from my high school days?" It felt safer not to start with Clark's visit to the hospital room.

"Who?"

"Clark Bradens. It took me a minute or so to recognize him, he's changed so much. I never thought *he'd* clean up his act. He's going to be fire chief when George retires next month, right?"

The mention wiped the smile from Dad's face. "So they say." He reached for the television remote.

She couldn't help herself. She wanted to know what had caused the strong reaction to Clark's visit at the hospital. "What's he like?"

"How would I know? I don't see that boy." He turned on the news and turned up the volume. The conversation had been declared over. She wasn't really surprised that Dad had said "that boy" with the same tone people had used to refer to Clark in high school. Usually around the phrase "stay away from that boy." Clark was no hero back then.

Melba was opening her mouth to try again when Barney pushed open the back door. "Lord, save me from church committees!" she declared as she shucked off her coat and set her handbag on the table. "A lot of good may get done, but a whole lot of not-good creeps in around the edges. Some town gossips ought to just hush up and stay home."

Melba left her dad to his television news and leaned against the kitchen doorway. "Tough day at the office?"

"Talk, whisper, talk. And then they wonder why the young people leave this town." Barney shook her head. "We've known for two weeks since the town council meeting, but the yammering hasn't stopped yet. You'd think there's never been a second chance given in the whole wide world the way some of them went on about Clark Bradens this afternoon. Ain't too many of us could stand up to judgment by who we was in high school." She gave out a trio of disapproving *tsk-tsk*s as she moved the casserole dish from the fridge to the oven.

"Clark Bradens? Why'd he come up?"

"Some folks want to throw him a nice party when George retires and he takes up as fire chief. I say it's a fine thing to celebrate a son coming home like that. Others, well…they don't see it that way. All they can see is a young high school punk coasting on his papa's coattails. Honestly." Melba wiped her hands on a dish-towel. "How many years has it been, and since when isn't a man allowed to grow up and get it right?"

"Who says he's grown up and gotten it right?" Melba could hardly believe Dad was standing behind her. He'd gotten up out of the recliner all on his own?

"He seemed nice enough to me."

"When'd you meet him?"

Dad was fine, Dad wasn't so fine. It was like living on an emotional Ping-Pong table. "I just told you I ran into him this morning." Her frustration ran away with her better sense, because she heard herself add, "You yelled at him last night when he brought me food in your hospital room."

"I couldn't have yelled at him. He'd have no business visiting me."

"I just said he was bringing *me* food. I met him in the hospital cafeteria and he offered to get Dellio's for me but a fire alarm made him late."

Dad shuffled into the kitchen and plopped himself down on the nearest chair. "He's going to be fire chief." He did not say it like a person pleased with the idea. In fact, his words had a "there goes the neighborhood" tone.

Melba started to say "We just talked about that," but shut her mouth in resignation. Instead, she caught Barney's eye over her father's head, and they shared a split second of silent concern.

"Did you really holler at that boy? Or rather, since he is older than your daughter, did you really holler at that *man?*" Barney asked.

"I just said I didn't yell at that Bradens boy," Dad snapped.

"Have the world your way, then." Barney huffed. It was what she said whenever Dad's version of the world didn't line up with reality. Melba hoped she'd someday acquire the ability to let it roll off her the way Barney did. "Get on out of this kitchen, you grumpy old man. Dinner won't be ready for another fifty minutes."

Melba reached out to help her father out of his chair, but he brushed her off. With considerable effort, Dad pushed himself up and shuffled, grumbling, back to the recliner. She stared after him and shook her head. "Should I be glad he's moving around, or annoyed at his mood?"

Barney laughed and pulled a package of brown-and-serve rolls out of the freezer. "Both."

Melba got a cookie sheet out of the cabinet and took the package from Barney. "He really did haul off at Clark in the hospital room," she said quietly as she broke apart the rolls and arranged them on the cookie sheet. "It was scary, actually. Came out of nowhere. He yelled at Clark like they knew each other."

Barney leaned back against the counter. "You know George Bradens and your father have never gotten along—not for a long time, anyway. Too easy to get a flood of bad water under the bridge in a small town like this. I heard they were close when they were younger."

A thought struck Melba. "Clark looks a lot like his dad, doesn't he?"

"With all that Bradens red hair, I expect he does. I ain't ever seen a photo of young George but I can picture it easy enough."

Melba moved closer. "Dad kept thinking I was Mom last night. Do you suppose he thought Clark was George, thought it was back then?"

"Could be."

"The question is, then, what could have happened in the past that made Dad so angry at George?"

"Who knows?" Barney nodded in the direction of the living room. "But take care, hon. Sometimes it don't pay to dig up past hurts like that."

Too late, Melba thought. *The digging's been started for me. Only I don't know if Dad realizes he's the one who picked up the shovel.*

Melba pulled on her robe and padded downstairs like a woman about to face the noose. She'd been up half the night, her mind a storm of questions about what her father had said at the hospital when they'd been alone. She'd tried to put it out of her mind, knowing Dad didn't want to talk about it. *Help me let it go,* she'd prayed nearly hourly since Dad had come home, but to no avail. With the thin pale rays of dawn came the realization that it could no longer be avoided.

She knew as she smelled coffee that there would never be a better time. He was up, sitting with coffee in his recliner. She was still up, having barely slept. And Barney wasn't due for another hour. *Give me the right words, Father. This is going to need so much grace and I'm running on empty.*

"Morning, Dad."

He turned toward her, and she marveled at the health in his features. He looked like Dad again, not that ghost of Dad who'd thrashed around his hospital bed. "Mornin' Melbadoll." He smiled, and she fought the urge to just let the day slide into peaceful normalcy.

It won't. It can't until you talk about this, she argued with herself while she fixed a cup of tea and dragged herself into the living room to perch on the ottoman by Dad's chair. "I need to ask you something, Dad."

He raised an eyebrow and sipped his coffee. "Shoot."

She'd rehearsed twelve ways to ask this, but couldn't think of one. "I know people say stuff when they're sick, and you had a high fever, but you said something to me in the hospital."

"Okay, maybe I could be nicer about that Bradens boy, but…"

"No, Dad, it doesn't have anything to do with that." She couldn't resist adding, "But yes, you could be nicer." She stirred her tea, trying to come up with the right words. "This is…something you said to me. Actually—" this hurt to say "—I think you thought you were talking to Mom, the way you said it." When his eyes grew anxious, she added, "You were pretty sick and on a lot of medication."

"You look so much like her." He said it with such tenderness, then shifted his gaze away from her to out the window.

"I like that, you know? It used to bug me in school when everyone would say, 'Oh, you must be Maria's daughter,' but I like it now." Melba squinted her eyes shut, pulling up a thread of courage from the place deep inside her chest that hadn't settled since the hospital. "Dad, you looked at me, called me Maria, and said 'She ought to know she's not mine.'"

Melba watched her father's body take in the words. Even with his face away from her, it was like a shock wave, hitting his shoulders, flinching his fingers, pushing on his chest. Part of her wanted him to not remember, to dismiss it as another of his "gone away" moments, but the telltale movements left no doubt. She was almost afraid for him to turn toward her.

When he did, his face was so full of pain and heartbreak it pummeled the breath from her lungs. "I didn't say that." It was a last-ditch denial.

"Yes, Dad, you did. And I think we should talk about it, don't you?"

He turned away from her again. The fingers around his coffee cup began to twitch. "I didn't say…" The coffee cup tumbled out of his grasp before she could catch it, spilling coffee on his lap. He yelped at the heat, the flash of anger she'd grown to fear surging up in him. "Don't give me hot coffee like that!" he snapped at her, forgetting it was he who'd served himself this morning. To think she'd been pleased at his self-sufficiency.

By the time Melba had gotten Dad cleaned up and calmed down, they were both exhausted and irritable. When she arrived, Barney's frown told Melba they looked as bad as they felt. Melba looked up from her third cup of tea as she clung to her last nerve while Dad shouted things at the news broadcasters from a too-loud television in the living room.

"Last night not go so well?" Barney said, nodding

toward the blasting news headlines on the other side of the kitchen door.

"No, the night went fine. This morning, not so much."

"Did he fall?"

"No. It's my fault. I tried to get him to explain something he said to me in the hospital and it…" Melba pushed out a breath that felt like concrete in her lungs. "It didn't go well." She hated that she felt tears twist up her throat. "He's so…here sometimes, and then the next second he's…" She swallowed, unable to come up with a suitable alternative to "gone."

Barney sat down. "I know," she said, putting a hand over Melba's. "This is hard. For you most of all. You gotta have faith God's going to walk you through this, and I know you do, but that don't mean it isn't tough to see some mornings." She frowned at Melba's face, asking, "How much sleep did you get last night?"

I must look a sight, Melba thought. She was still in her pajamas and hadn't put her contacts in or brushed her hair. "Not a whole lot."

Barney patted Melba's hand. "Why don't you go upstairs and nap a bit. I'll take care of Mr. Personality in there and see if I can't lighten the mood."

"Actually—" Melba stifled a yawn "—I think the best thing for me would be a run. A little sunshine and fresh air ought to do me a world of good."

"Never could see the point in that, but if that's your ticket, then by all means. Go burn off stress."

"Burn off chocolate cake, actually." Melba was surprised to find a smile creep onto her lips. Nothing was going to solve itself anytime soon, so she was going to have to learn to cope while knee-deep in uncertainty.

Uncertainty over what to think, what to do, where to find the answers she sought. And most of all, uncertainty over how to deal with the revelation that she was now certain was true—that Dad wasn't her father after all. She needed time to think, to pray, to start pulling at all those knots in front of her, and she did that best while running.

Chapter Four

Chad Owens kept jogging. "Forget about it. What do a bunch of old ladies know?"

Clark held out a hand to halt Chad's steps as they jogged together on the river bank path. He wanted Chad to take more offense at what he'd just heard. "Those old ladies know how to make a fuss, how to complain to other people, and probably how to write letters to the editor of the town newspaper. I'm going to pay for the fact that they aren't happy about the idea of me as fire chief."

Chad shook his head and kept running. "The town council's already voted. You're already hired. You're in uniform. You formally take over in a month. It's just noise."

"I go to that church." Clark dashed to catch up. "I spent three hours mopping out the basement from the last flood. Why do they still think of me as some kind of hooligan?"

Now it was Chad who stopped. "You can't tell me you didn't see this coming." He wiped his forehead with one sleeve. "You didn't exactly leave here Prince

Charming. Did you think everyone would come around in the first month?"

Clark didn't really have an answer. "I suppose I figured once the hiring became official, that'd be the end of it."

Chad put one leg up on the park bench beside him and stretched a calf muscle. "Come on, Clark, I didn't even grow up here and I could have told you this was going to happen." He looked straight at Clark. "You have some pretty big fire boots to fill."

"Tell me about it."

Chad cuffed Clark's shoulder. "He's been fire chief around here for ages. You'd constitute a big change even if you were identical to him."

It wasn't much of a help.

"And you're completely different from him," Chad continued as he stretched the other leg.

Clark started running again. "Thanks for the vote of confidence there."

"Hang on." Chad caught up. "What I'm trying to say is this is an uphill battle no matter who steps in as chief, so don't worry about a little bit of friction."

"Oh, so I suppose that's why you didn't step up to take over as chief? Didn't want to take the hit but happy to watch me go down in flames?" Clark didn't really feel that way, but life didn't offer up too many chances to rib Chad Owens, so he had to find his targets when he could. It had gotten a bit easier since he'd married just before Clark came back to town.

"I'm too busy to be chief."

"Too busy playing the happy newlywed. You've put on a few pounds being married to the candy store lady."

Chad smirked. He smirked a lot more since his wife,

Jeannie, and stepson, Nick, had come into his life, and Clark was truly happy for the guy. "I can handle it. And what about you?"

"Oh, that's the last thing I need right now. I've got to play the straight-and-narrow for a while. One hundred percent work and no social entanglements for the first six months, that's my plan."

"Funny thing about plans…" Chad said.

"Yeah, yeah, I've heard it before, but this is Gordon Falls. I'm safe. I've been here three weeks and so far the only single woman I've met is Melba Wingate." He tried to put disinterest in his voice, but the truth was Melba's chocolate-brown eyes and cascades of hair entered his memory far too easily.

Chad turned and jogged backwards in front of him, raising a teasing eyebrow. "Melba Wingate, huh?"

Clark reached out and nearly pushed him over. "Her dad's sick—she's got enough on her plate. And besides, you know I don't go for the artsy, esoteric types."

Chad stumbled but caught his footing. "I seem to remember athletic blondes being your specialty. In alarming numbers."

"Before," Clark corrected a bit too sharply, but it was a sore spot and Chad knew it.

"Before you cleaned up your act." Chad stopped and caught Clark's shoulder. "And you have. Look, you've pulled the biggest U-turn of anyone I know, Clark. I respect that. Everyone else will, too, you just have to give them time to see the change I've seen. Come on, even your dad came around. You're supposed to be here. Some old stories from who you were ten years ago aren't going to change that."

It was as much of a speech as Clark had ever heard

from Chad. He clasped Chad's hand on his shoulder, thankful for their friendship. "Thanks." Before things got too gooey, he ducked under Clark's arm and started running at a faster pace. "But you're still fat and married."

"Yeah, well, you're still skinny and obsessive."

"Lean and focused," he called as he turned a corner of the riverside path, "lean and focused." He turned back to see Chad was not following him. "What?"

"I'm done for the morning. You take that final mile on your own."

Clark pumped his fists in the air victoriously. "Because I *can*."

"Because you *need to*. See you at the station at two for the meeting with P.A. Crimson." They had a meeting with a safety equipment company that afternoon— Chad was seeing to it that Clark met all the vendors and suppliers.

Clark began thinking of all the ways he could kid Chad for "going soft" as he kept running. It wasn't hard; Chad was an easy target these days. Once a somber, serious loner, Chad had fallen hard—and completely against his will—for Jeannie Nelworth and her young son. Now the three of them were the poster family for happy endings, all sugary happiness and love-struck smiles. It was nice, in a make-your-teeth-hurt kind of way. Chad had known a lot of pain in his life, had lost a fiancée to a fire and shut down for too many years. It was fun to rib him for his newfound light-heartedness.

The perfect taunt had just come to Clark, and he was actually laughing out loud as he turned a corner on the jogging path and nearly tripped over Melba Wingate. She was sitting on the path clutching one ankle and he almost tumbled over top of her but managed to catch himself to stumble alongside.

"Whoa….you okay?"

Melba looked up at him with the same eyes he'd seen that first night at the hospital. Strained, weary, hanging on by a thread. And now, physical pain laced her expression as well. "That depends on your definition," she winced.

"Well, then, let's see." Melba watched Clark kick into first-responder mode, tugging at the sweatshirt now tied around his waist to wipe the sweat from his forehead. He crouched down beside her, lifted her ankle and gently removed her shoe, then tucked the bunched-up sweatshirt under her leg to cushion her foot as he set it back down. She tried not to wince, but ended up sucking in her breath sharply when he ran an assessing hand over her throbbing ankle.

"Ouch." She hated how weak and wobbly her voice sounded. She hated that she was on the verge of tears. Not because her leg hurt that much—although it was painful—but because it was a last straw of sorts. She'd thought the run would clear her head of her problems, but all it did was add another one on top. One more ding in an already battered-feeling life.

"No break, but you're swelling a bit. I'd say 'ouch' is justified."

Somehow, it was the exact wrong thing to say. Melba's fragile emotions took it as permission to overflow. She tried to hold it back, but a small sob escaped from her tight throat. *This is a really bad place to lose it,* she told herself, but the admonition only made things worse. She looked away, pointlessly trying to hide the tears that stole disobediently down her face.

"Hey." Clark's voice dropped its clinical tone completely. The warmth of it only made things worse. That kind of tone always got to her these days. The best nurses in Dad's hospital—the ones for whom crisis caring was a true gift, not just a job—could bring on tears just with a hand on her shoulder. "Whoa there, you just turned an ankle, you'll be…" He stopped and sat down beside her. "Well, I was gonna say 'fine' but I think maybe that's the wrong word here." He paused for a moment before asking, "Running from, huh?"

"What?" His odd question made her turn and look at him. It broke the tension of trying to keep her emotions in check—there was no hiding the tears once she turned. There had been no hiding them earlier, really, but the trick served to loosen the knot in her throat. Clark's eyes were full of compassion, without a hint of judgment. Why must Clark Bradens always find her at the end of her rope?

He sighed and rested his elbows on his knees, as if ready to stay a while. "My fire chief in Detroit said that when you run, it's best to know if you're running *to* or running *from*. He had a theory that you never got hurt running to something, you got hurt running from something." It was an odd thing to notice at the moment, but Melba could see that rescuing was deep in Clark's nature. The urge to help—either here or at the hospital vending machine or on the street corner yesterday— seemed to leap from him without effort. This Clark was a bit of a shock—it felt so much at odds with the careless trouble-seeker the high school Clark had been.

"From." She pointed to her ankle, surprised to find

a damp little laugh bubbling up from the tide of tears. "The theory holds."

"That's been my experience." He offered a half-hearted shrug. "Done my share of 'running from,' too."

Melba waited for Clark to ask her what she was running from, but he didn't. They sat there for a moment, quiet amid the pale green of the Gordon River's waking spring. She hadn't even noticed before now that it was a pretty morning; her thoughts had been inwardly focused. The chief's theory made plain and painful sense. She sighed and flexed her foot, feeling foolish. It startled her that some part of her wanted Clark to pry, to give her an excuse to blurt out the storm of questions brewing inside her. They wouldn't surface on their own—raw and deep as the pain and uncertainty were—but they wanted to be pulled out of her. Running from. It seemed almost inevitable now that she tripped and turned her ankle.

Clark picked up a twig and began spinning it in his fingers. "You've got a lot chasing you."

It was a perfectly phrased comment, opening the door for her to say more but not requiring it. The urge to tell him everything—to open up about leaving Chicago and the torture of her fading father, about disappointment and postponed travel plans and the bone-deep suspicion that she wasn't who she thought she was—pushed at her like a sudden squall. The tears burned behind her eyes again. "Yeah." It was a gulped whisper, a last-ditch effort to hold it all in. She nodded—twice—rather than attempt any more words.

"This whole parent thing, the coming back when you're not a kid anymore, it's rough. The roles get all tangled. Add your dad's…condition…and, well, it'd be easy to see how ankles get turned." Clark shifted himself down toward her foot again. "Flex it and see how it feels."

She did. "It hurts less now."

He looked back up at her with something close to the charming wink she remembered from high school. "See, better already." He'd been bad-boy hunky as a teen; a flame of too-long red hair that tumbled behind him as he tore through town helmetless on a loud motorcycle. Now, his short hair and stunning features were strong rather than wild. He was as handsome as ever, but in a completely different manner. And far too appealing for someone already struggling with more than she could handle.

He stilled for a moment, as if deciding whether or not to say something. The same hesitation she'd seen at the coffee shop when she asked him about his accident. "Not too many people our age here to talk to. Not who get what it's like to come back. It's kind of a tight fit to squeeze back into Gordon Falls, don't you think?"

Melba merely nodded again, the squall pushing harder. Clark felt so easy to talk to. He was an outsider newly forced in, just like she was. It'd be so simple to let it all spill out of her on the quiet of the riverbank. How much she wanted one other soul on earth to know she hadn't imagined what her father blurted out in his delusion. Clark had no stake in the secret. He'd been a dangerous young man; he probably had a closetful of past secrets himself. Melba ventured a long look at him, noting that his green eyes had a singed quality around the edges. He had secrets and scars. Melba's forefinger found Dad's wedding band still on her thumb and tried on the thought of betraying the secret to just one other person.

"It's hard," she managed. How many times had she said that phrase lately? "He's…" She couldn't think of a way to start, and wasn't even sure she should start at all. There was an odd, tenuous space between them— too close and yet too far apart at the same time.

"Everybody loves your dad," Clark said after a moment, his eyes returning to a professional assessment of her ankle as his warm fingers tested muscle and joint. "They were praying for him in church while he was in the hospital and Barney told me people have been by to help."

"Sure, now. What about weeks from now when he's still sick? Sicker."

"The help will still be there. Honestly, you'll probably get more help than you need, the way folks like to poke their noses in around here." He looked up at her again as he reached for her running shoe. "It's going to be okay."

His eyes were intense, focused, compelling. She had a vision of him reaching a victim in a cloud of smoke, extending a hand, saying those words with the same lure of confidence he exuded now. Trouble was, Clark only saw part of the fire burning around her—the disease, the logistical challenge. He had no idea of the full-blown firestorm licking at her heels. How she wasn't the least bit sure it was going to be okay ever again.

It wasn't his problem. It wasn't fair to make it his problem, either.

Melba took the shoe, stuffing the urge to tell all back

down with the same effort she forced her swollen ankle back into its shoe.

Both hurt far too much.

Chapter Five

Charlotte Taylor was a sight for sore eyes. Melba hugged the stuffing out of her coworker and best friend as she got off the train in Gordon Falls. "I'm so glad to see you!"

Charlotte, who was an urban girl to the core, spun around on her black leather boots to squint at the little train station with her mouth open. "Wow, girl, you live in a postcard. I feel like I'm on a movie set." She nudged Melba. "You grew up in this place? Really?"

It was a funny thing, living in a place like Gordon Falls. People thought of it as peaceful and perfect, not at all ready to think of it as having bumps and warts like any other community. "Mom used to say Gordon Falls was like a duck swimming upstream. Peaceful and charming on the surface, furiously paddling with big clumsy feet underneath."

Her words must have had more of an edge than she realized, for Charlotte dropped her overnight bag and took Melba by both shoulders. "That bad already?" she said quietly. Charlotte had lost her grandfather to Alzheimer's two years ago, and as such she'd become Melba's go-to shoulder to cry on. Just the look in Charlotte's eyes returned the lump to Melba's throat.

She shook it off, picking up Charlotte's bag and putting an arm around her friend instead. "Yes and no. I've got an hour before we have to be home, so let's go introduce you to some excellent apple pie."

"Pie. This really is a movie set. We're riding in an actual car, aren't we? Not a horse and buggy?"

Charlotte was the kind of friend who could make Melba laugh even in the worst of circumstances, which was exactly why she'd called her to come out for an overnight visit. Besides, she knew the daily life of Alzheimer's, so Melba felt comfortable bringing her to the house where she still wasn't comfortable with lots of company yet. Dad could be so unpredictable, and not everyone could handle that. "My car is right there. We're quaint, but not that quaint."

Charlotte tucked herself into the passenger seat. "I half worried I'd find you in a bonnet and apron or something."

Melba rolled her eyes. "I went ninety miles down the interstate, Charlotte, not back in time."

Turning to look at her for a long assessment, Charlotte sighed. "You look tired. How are you holding up?"

"Some parts are okay, others have been…" Melba didn't know how or where to begin. "…startling." She put the car in gear. "You know what it's like."

"Still, it hits everyone different. It hits every *day* different." Charlotte reached out a fingerless-gloved hand to give Melba's shoulder a squeeze. "I'm glad you called. You need backup to do this. It's just too nuts to handle alone. I have Mom, but for you…well, it's *just you.*"

"I have Barney. And a month's worth of church casseroles." Melba seized the chance to talk about something happy. "How—and where—is Mima?"

"Oh, you know Mima." Charlotte exhaled. Her grandmother had taken life by the horns after her husband's long decline, and become a world traveler. "Where's Mima?" had become a grown-up version of the children's search book *Where's Waldo?* at Melba's office. Half of Melba's yearning to travel the world had been nurtured by Mima's tales of adventure. "Indonesia at the moment, then home for the holidays, then I think it's Greenland."

Melba laughed. "Greenland? Why?"

Charlotte shrugged her shoulders, setting her long blond hair swinging. "Why not?"

"Your grandmother never did need a reason."

Charlotte whipped out her ever-present smartphone, fingers flying. "I'm sending her a message right now, asking her to flood you with postcards. What's your address here in Charmingland?"

"Mima texts?"

"Mima is a thoroughly modern woman. I bought her a smartphone for her birthday."

Melba gave the address as she pulled into Cafe Homestead, informing her friend that it was the purveyor of the state's most delicious apple pie as well as an impressive selection of tea. Life felt a bit more in place now—good tea and a good friend made a world of difference.

An hour later, pie consumed, introductions made, and Dad happily dozing in front of the television set, Melba and Charlotte sat across from each other on the bed in Melba's room. Melba leaned back against the headboard and fingered the eyelet lace on a yellow throw pillow left over from her teenage years. "I feel like I'm fifteen and having a sleepover," she said, staring around at her once-beloved butter-colored walls and cream curtains.

Charlotte ran her hands through the fringe on one of the fabrics Melba had draped over those cream curtains. "It's like you just spread the Melba I know overtop a lemon meringue pie or something." She laughed when Melba moaned. "No, it's sort of fun. I bet you thought this was fab-u-lous when you were that age."

"It's a bit weird to me now. It's home, but then again it's foreign territory. Like the layers won't fit together right anymore." She caught a photograph of her and her mother—a sunny, smiling scene from a visit home just after she'd moved to Chicago—and felt her throat tighten.

Charlotte rolled over to perch on her elbows. "Okay, we've done all the preliminary niceties, so why don't you tell me what's up?"

Melba swallowed hard. "I thought this would be easier, you know? Like a list of tasks or coordinating medications or just being around." It was the tip of the iceberg—the big, dangerous emotional iceberg waiting to sink her Titanic—but she couldn't think of another place to start.

Charlotte's smile held the edge of remembered pain—her grandparents had lived with her right up until the end. "It's hard stuff. Taking care of Grandpa was like going to war some days. With an enemy you can't see or predict or even fight. You can only duck out of the way and hope you survive."

The metaphor seemed to offer a way to say the un-thinkable out loud. "I didn't duck, and I've already been hit." The tears came out of nowhere, like they seemed to too often these days. "A big bomb dropped on me, Charlotte, and I don't know what to do about it."

Charlotte scrambled across the bedspread to pull Melba into a fierce hug. "Yeah, you did know what to do. You called me. We saved the Colorado Alpaca Fleece account, girl, and that means we can tackle just about anything."

Somehow pacifying an irate alpaca fleece supplier whose product had been mislabeled—twice—didn't seem a match for what Dad had dumped on her, but Melba let the feisty energy of Charlotte's hug soothe her soul. She cried on her friend's go-to shoulder for a minute or so, then pushed her hair out of her eyes. "That was a monster of a problem, wasn't it? This problem is a bit harder to solve, though. This bomb has…real damage potential."

Charlotte sat up. "Okay, start at the beginning."

Pulling her knees up to hug them, Melba let the words crawl out, small and vulnerable. "Well, you know Dad got pretty sick last week, and his mind sort of… short-circuited."

"Good way to put it," Charlotte sighed. "I always thought 'dementia' sounded so gruesome."

"He said some things. One thing, actually, that was a big shocker." Melba steeled herself with a deep breath, sure it would make the thing more awful to hear it spoken out loud. "He said…he said I wasn't his." There. She'd said it and not melted into the carpeting.

It took Charlotte a few excruciating moments to

grasp what Melba was saying. "You mean, not his daughter? *Biologically?*"

Melba could only nod. It was so much more complicated than biology.

"Really? I mean, you're sure? You said he wasn't himself—maybe he didn't know what he was saying."

"He knew what he was saying." Melba let her head fall back against the headboard. "He just didn't know he was saying it to *me*. He thought he was talking to Mom. He keeps mixing me up with her, talking to me like I was her. Then all of a sudden he yelled at me—at Mom—for making him keep it a secret. Said 'she'—meaning me—ought to know, that it was wrong I didn't know." She managed to drag her gaze up to look at Charlotte's startled blue eyes. "He talked as if he'd wanted to tell me for years—which means *he's known* for years—but Mom wouldn't allow it."

"Calling that a big shocker is an understatement. I think that qualifies as earth-shattering."

New tears sprung up in Melba's eyes. It did feel earth-shattering. As if everything around her had shifted off its foundations and cracked into pieces. Only no one else could see the destruction. She tried to say something, recapture the margins she'd drawn around the secret, but it had spiraled out of her grasp. "It's such a huge lie. And for so long. Why? Why do that to me? Why do that to anyone?" The tears surged up out of her control again. Sadness, and a sharp edge of anger she hadn't even realized was there. "I feel like this is eating me alive, and I don't even know for sure."

"You need to know. You've got to. I mean, how can you do anything at all until you know for sure?"

"How am I supposed to do that?"

Charlotte scooted up to sit next to her, throwing one arm around Melba's shoulders. Stretching out her long legs to cross them at the ankles, Melba heard Charlotte's "take action" voice kick in. Charlotte was a consummate problem solver, creative and rarely ruffled. "There's got to be a dozen ways to check this out." Her brows knit together and the fingers of one hand drummed against her thigh. "Only now that I think about it, you ought to ask yourself—do you *really* need to know?"

Melba glared at her. "Of course I need to know. You just *said* I need to know."

"I know I said that, but, Melba, does it change anything?"

"It changes everything. My dad's not my dad!" Melba felt like she wanted to throw something, to hurl anything within reach at the wall of doubt that had just risen up in front of her life.

Charlotte shifted to look into Melba's eyes with a serious expression. "That's not true. Your dad is still the father you've known. Mort has been your father your whole life. He loves you and you love him. The only thing that's changed is…well…genetics."

"And truth."

"Oh, kiddo." Charlotte sighed, her eyes softening, "I don't mean to be negative, but we all know how this trip ends. Given the little time you may have left with your dad, does it change a lot of who he was for you? Who he *is* to you?"

"I don't know. I feel like I don't know anything anymore. My history's been yanked out from under me like…like Dad's memory." The thought was poignant and painful in extremes.

"I take it you've asked him."

Melba shrugged deeper into the nest of yellow pillows. "Oh, and that went well. Denied the whole incident, when I think he actually did remember it. Some little bit of panic around the edge of his eyes told me he knew exactly what I was talking about. Then he spilled his coffee and it all tailspinned into a rant—as things tend to do now. Using Alzheimer's as an out? Who sanctioned that?"

Charlotte laughed. "Who sanctioned that?" was a favorite declaration of their boss when someone made a choice she didn't agree with. Startled at her own ability to still crack a joke, Melba found herself laughing a little bit, too. And then a lot. A burst of healing giggles that seemed to untangle the knot of stress in her chest. "See?" Charlotte said as she used a tissue to salvage what was left of her mascara. "You're still in there somewhere. You're still you."

"Am I?" It was an enormous question to hang on two little words.

"Yes, you are." Charlotte's eyes squinted up in problem-solving mode. "What's something you used to like doing with your dad? Something you could still do now?"

Melba had to think. "I've spent so much brain power on everything he can't do anymore, I hadn't even thought about what he can do. It's not much."

Charlotte jumped off the bed to circle the room, as if scanning for clues. "Can he walk?"

"As long as it's not far."

"Any favorite spots?"

"Everyone loves the river here, but that's hardly…"

It hit her like a happy lightning bolt, a surge of warm memory. "Ducks."

Charlotte turned. "Ducks?"

"We loved feeding the ducks when I was a kid. We even did it once after Mom's funeral. He loves to feed the ducks down on the riverbank."

Charlotte pointed a finger at Melba with a wide smile. "We need to feed the ducks, then. You, me and your dad. Tomorrow." She showed her lifetime-city-dweller status when she raised a blond eyebrow and asked, "What do ducks eat?"

"We always fed them the heels of bread loaves."

The eyebrow arched farther. "The what?"

Melba laughed, the sensation warm and expansive and infinitely welcome. "Where did you grow up? Bread heels? The crusty end pieces nobody wants?"

Charlotte blinked. "You're not supposed to eat those?"

It was a full two seconds before Melba registered that Charlotte was toying with her. She flung a pillow at her friend. "You're impossible." A second and third pillow followed. "I'm so glad you're here."

"You want to take her out for the afternoon?" Max Jones dangled the boat keys in front of Clark with a knowing smile.

"I expect I'll only need an hour." The boat was in pristine shape with lovely lines. While chief was one of only two paid positions in the large volunteer fire department—Chad's being the other—the salary wasn't huge. Clark was glad he had savings enough to consider the boat when he'd heard Max was selling it. Jones had taken excellent care of her, and Clark doubted it would take more than fifteen minutes on the river to sell him on the craft.

Max grinned. "So take two. By the way," he called over his shoulder as he walked back up the dock steps toward the riverfront kayak shop he owned, "I heard if you go up around the bend by the bridge, your cell service drops off the planet. Just in case you're looking to disappear."

As if to force the issue, Clark's cell phone buzzed in his pocket. The fifth text message this hour, two from Dad. For a man who claimed to be "old-fashioned," George Bradens had taken to texting with entirely too much enthusiasm. Even the younger firefighters had started joking about getting "Gexts," friendly "just checkin' up" texts from Chief George. Technology had handed the chief a new way to meddle, and Clark moaned in regret as he flipped open his phone to read some unimportant detail that surely could have waited. "Just beyond the bend, huh?"

"Works every time!" Max shouted from the door of his shop.

Alone, on the water, in a beautiful boat, out of cell service. It sounded like an hour or two of bliss. Worth emptying his entire savings, not just the large chunk of it the boat would cost. *Thanks, Lord, for knowing just what I needed today,* Clark prayed as he hopped into the driver's seat and started the engine. The deep, gurgling sound of an outboard motor on the river filled his heart immediately. Nothing spoke of home and peace to Clark like time on the river. Despite the enormous lake right in front of the city, he'd somehow managed to feel land-locked in Detroit. As he cast off the dock lines, Clark felt like he had flung bindings off his own lungs that he didn't even know were there. Here, churning the river underneath him, was the antidote for the tight squeeze of Gordon Falls. This would be his escape, the valve that would allow him to let off steam when the pressures of work and small-town life got to him. As he pulled away from the dock, the whole thing seemed so much more doable, so much less overwhelming than it had even an hour ago. *You knew,* Clark mused with his eyes toward heaven. When he'd caught wind of the boat for sale, he could think of nothing else. The fact that the name on the back of the boat was "Escape Clause" practically sealed the deal.

Slicing through the river's gentle current, Clark felt the world expand around him. Space and grace as far as the eye could see. Gordon Falls was a pretty town from the street, but she was stunning from the river. Even in the muted colors of spring, with mud everywhere and things just beginning to bud, Clark felt himself fall a little bit back in love with the town he'd grown to hate as an angry teenager. The town he'd fled at the first possible opportunity. The town that, in less than a month, he'd be sworn in to protect as fire chief.

Within the space of fifteen minutes, Clark felt himself grinning in the pale afternoon sunshine as he pushed the throttle to send the boat faster. On this small river, he couldn't set off at wild speeds like some sort of ocean race boat, but the wind tumbling through his hair was energizing. The stress blew off him, sloughing off his spirit to sink in the white foam of his wake. Like the motorcycles of his youth but yet altogether different. Pulse-racingly perfect.

Until he heard the shouting from somewhere over his left shoulder.

Clark pulled himself out of his waterborne stupor to see a tiny calamity erupting on the riverbank. Two women trying to hold back an old man who was shouting and waving. He throttled back the boat to realize the old man was railing against him. It had been years since he'd heard any version of the "you speed-loving hooligan" shout but the recognition was instantaneous. What took a few seconds longer to process was the shock that the old man was standing in two feet of icy April river—and that the old man was Mort Wingate.

Chapter Six

Clark cut the engine back as far as possible while still turning the boat towards the commotion. Within ten seconds he was close enough to hear Melba's frantic and embarrassed voice. "For goodness' sake, Dad, come out of the water right now!"

"What's the matter with you? Can't a man feed the ducks in peace without some idiot racing down the river like there's no tomorrow?" For an old, sick man, Mort was putting up a pretty good fight. The women couldn't hold him back, and he'd gained another couple of inches into the water toward the boat as he kept shouting.

"Sorry!" Clark yelled, although it seemed useless. Melba and her friend were in the river up to their knees now, shouting and pulling on Mort's waving arms. One slip and the three of them would be under the chilly waters—he couldn't think of anything else to do but gun the engine and bring the boat up on shore beside them.

"Dad!" Melba shouted as Mort came right for Clark, who vaulted out of the boat in a splash of shockingly cold water and made the shore in three strides. Thankfully, his split-second plan worked, for Mort came right at him.

"You selfish rat! Don't give a thought for anyone else around you, do you?"

"Sir…"

"Don't you 'sir' me, you good-for-nothing…"

"Dad!" Melba's voice was a shriek as Mort tripped. He would have landed full in the water had Clark not caught him at the last minute.

For whatever reason, the shock of nearly falling snapped Mort out of his rage. While he didn't exactly calm, his tirade subsided. He pushed himself off Clark with a brusque, feisty anger and stomped up the river-bank, grumbling something Clark couldn't make out. He was pretty sure he was better off not hearing.

"We should call an ambulance," the blonde woman said more calmly than he would have thought.

"No," Melba shot back. "I can get him home."

Clark doubted that. In another split-second decision, he took off his jacket and tossed his cell phone to the blonde. "Hit speed-dial two…it'll connect you to the fire station. Ask for Jesse Sykes and tell him to bring three rescue blankets." He tossed the jacket to Melba, who was trying to guide her father to a nearby bench. "See if you can get this on him while I tie the boat up. I'd take his pulse, but I don't think he'd let me near him."

Mort glared at him, but it was a wounded, confused glare, which softened just a bit as Melba threw his coat over her father's now-shivering shoulders. The look in the old man's eyes told Clark even Mort himself wasn't quite sure what had just happened. What an awful, tor-mented way to feel, Clark thought as he tugged the boat firmly up on the shore. To lose chunks of yourself right in front of your own eyes. *I'd yell at someone, too.*

By the time Jesse showed up with blankets, Melba and Charlotte—he'd learned the blonde's name by then—had maneuvered an exhausted Mort into Melba's car. Melba was spent, too. He watched her put her head down on the car roof for a weary second after shutting the backseat door.

"Here," he said, picking up the sorry bag of old bread he'd found by the water's edge. "I'm sorry I ruined your outing."

"Duck feeding." She rolled her eyes and shrugged her shoulders. "I don't know what I was thinking." The futility in her tone cut into Clark's gut.

"You were trying to have a nice moment with your dad." Clark nodded back toward the boat. "A nice quiet moment I sort of…made impossible."

"It's not your fault. I don't know why he did that." She pulled her own coat closer around her. "I don't know why he does much of anything anymore."

Clark fought the urge to put a hand on her shoulder. "Are you all going to be okay?"

"That's the million-dollar question, isn't it?"

"Charlotte seems like a cool head in a tight spot."

Melba glanced back at her friend, who was trying to engage Mort in friendly conversation in the car as if they'd just gone out for ice cream instead of staging a drama in icy river waters. "Charlotte? She's great backup. She lost her grandfather to Alzheimer's two years ago. She knows the drill."

"It's good to have backup." There was a weird silence between them. He had the sensation of having seen too much of her life exposed. The awkwardness of knowing more than he ought to. It pulled at him, as did the astounding velvet-brown of her eyes, in ways that seemed so unwise. "Everybody needs backup."

She noticed the shiver than ran down his back. In fact, his wet feet were so insanely cold they hurt. "And you need your coat back."

She turned for the car door, but he caught her elbow. "No." The moment, the touch, burned between them as if someone had just lit a torch. For a moment Clark forgot what he was going to say. Forgot the pins of pain attacking his soggy feet. Forgot why Melba Wingate was the perfect example of how he was so easily distracted. "You…um…just hang on to it for now." He had to send a very specific mental command to his hand to unwrap itself from the tiny span of her forearm. "I'd see you all home, but I have to get this boat back. It's not even mine—well, not yet, anyways. I'll come by the house later this afternoon and make sure everyone's okay. I can get it back then."

She held up a cautionary hand. "I don't think…"

"I'll call your cell first to see if it's a good time. You know, if he's sleeping or something so I won't get him all riled up again. I suspect he's exhausted from all this."

She pushed her hair back off her face again. "I know I am." It was clear that she was hanging on by a thread when she did that. Under siege and yet courageous at the same time. It did something to him—pulled out urges to comfort and protect—that no amount of cautionary thinking could undo.

"Sometime around four, okay?"

"Yeah, that's good. Barney'll be there making dinner—she can keep an eye on Dad." She fished into her coat pocket for her car keys.

"Hey." He waited until she looked up at him. "I'll show up this time. Promise."

That got a smile from her. "Like my Dellio's?"

"Tell you what—I'll take you to Dellio's and you can order whatever fungus you want." That wasn't the smartest of ideas, but he'd just ruined a quiet afternoon she'd probably planned for days with her dad. Exacerbating her problems was becoming a bad habit, even if he had no idea how he kept doing so. It was time he got something right in this town.

She hesitated. "Clark…"

Her near-sigh of his name was a fatal mistake. "Well, now you've done it. You take a man with hero tendencies—a firefighter, for example—you let him mess up on you not once but twice, and then you say his name like that? 'No' just left the list of viable options." The fragile smile that crept across her face finished the job her sigh had started. He smiled and pointed at her. "I'll see you at four."

Melba should have stopped eating French fries twenty fries ago. "Are you going to buy that boat?"

Clark leaned back against the red vinyl booth as some 1950s baritone launched into another crooning oldies ballad. "I already did. Paid Max right there and then when I brought it back."

"After everything that happened on the riverbank?" She hadn't had "small talk" since forever, so she was grateful that Clark had kept the conversation away from Dad and their dramatic afternoon. But sooner or later, one of them had to bring it up. The elephant in the room couldn't be ignored forever.

"I figure that boat and I have a history now."

How did he do that? Treat such calamity as if it were amusing rather than unnerving?

"You make it sound like you couldn't have planned a more entertaining afternoon." The words came out with a tone of hurt she didn't even realize was lurking inside. She had *wanted* it to be an entertaining afternoon, had hoped that it would be. She hadn't realized Charlotte's idea had sprung such a longing for the relationship she used to have with her father.

Clark doused his enormous hamburger with more ketchup. You could barely make out the fries under the red sea he'd already poured on them. "It will be a funny story. Just maybe not for another six years or so."

"He'll be long gone by then." She gave a little gasp, surprised something so morbid had blurted out of her. Melba glanced up at Clark, expecting to see the same shock she felt, but his eyes were steady. An "it's okay" silently reflected in their warm sadness. "Well, maybe not," she covered with false cheer.

Clark set the ketchup bottle down. "Do you know how long he has?" His question had a careful, quiet tone. "Have they given you any idea?" Melba swallowed hard, and he broke off his gaze. "I'm sorry, that's none of my business, is it?"

"No, it's just that no one's been…" it took her a second to find the right word "…brave enough to ask me that. Everyone talks around it, hints at it, but they never really ask. I mean, who wants to hear *that* answer?" She picked at a stray sesame seed that had fallen off her bun. "But I have to acknowledge it. It's all I can ever think about, most days." It was so much more than that. It touched every thought, every action, made everything that wasn't about Dad—like having Dellio's with Clark

Bradens—feel selfish and wrong. Now had to be all about Dad, because maybe now was all she'd ever have.

Clark leaned forward a bit. She'd spent the last five minutes thinking his eyes couldn't get any more intense, but she'd been wrong. "How do you think about it? I mean, how do you get your head around something so big as that?"

Melba didn't really know how to explain it. This wasn't like a work project, where she'd make a conscious decision to tackle a massive challenge. "It's like having a ten-ton weight dumped on you a fraction at a time. You know it's there, you see hints of it for a while and you pretend not to notice. You tell yourself it's not really that heavy. Then something…cracks…and the whole ten tons of it falls around your ankles." The metaphors seemed dumb and inaccurate, but it did feel good to at least try and put the experience into words. "I'm stuck trying to figure out how to live among the pieces, I suppose. Only they don't hold together anymore, and I can feel the time running out between them. Like a leak you can't stop." She hadn't planned on saying so much, but Clark's eyes had a way of making her ease up on the tight grip she held around herself.

"I don't think I'm the brave one at this table. I don't know how you do it." Melba had been the target of many sad gazes in the past weeks, but Clark's held a glow of admiration beside the compassion. Pity was comforting, but admiration—his admiration—felt like it relit the fuel of her determination. "I'd be begging God to get me out of that every hour if I were in your shoes. I'm not wired for that sort of thing, but you? You manage it, even when it seems impossible. If I had one of those plastic hero badges we give out to the second graders

I'd pin twelve of them on you this minute." He blinked, then ran his hands down his face. "I think that was the goofiest thing I've ever said to anyone."

It was goofy, but it touched a part of her that had been squeezed tight for weeks. The resulting laugh felt welcome and filled with grace. "No, it's sweet." When he raised a red eyebrow from behind his hands, she added, "In a weird, off-beat kind of way." Melba took a deep breath, feeling the tension slough off her shoulders. "Thanks."

Clark leaned on one elbow. "For complimenting you with twelve plastic badges?"

"For this." Then, to her surprise, she added, "For dragging me out of the house." She shook her head, remembering the chaos of the afternoon. "For dragging Dad out of the water."

"Hero tendencies. I like to save people. I just prefer to do it on dry land or I'd have joined the Coast Guard."

"Well, you did just buy a very pretty boat."

"Noticed those fine lines, did you? I ought to turn myself in for highway robbery. Max Jones sold it to me for a song."

He looked at Melba for a long second, his eyes slanted in decision. "I'd take you back out on her, but…" His eyes squinted shut for a moment. "Well, I'm not so sure that would be a smart thing to do."

No, that wasn't at all a smart thing to do. "No, thanks, I've already gotten wet."

"And I've already proven my weakness for…shall we say 'distractions.'" His eyes dropped to the checked tablecloth, his fingers nervously outlining the red squares. "Truth is, I made myself a promise when I came here, and I've already shown myself up for how bad I'll be at keeping it. I don't have the best track record for keeping my mind on my job. I just bought a boat named 'Escape Clause,' if you need an example." He looked up for a second, but couldn't hold her gaze in the same intense way he had a while ago. "I think that's one of the things God is trying to teach me in coming here. I need to put all my energy into being chief. Pop's put a lot of faith in me, and I need to earn it."

At any other time in her life, Melba would have been hurt, or at least annoyed at his unspoken "we can't take this any further," but his honesty—and her relief—wouldn't let her. He was admitting he felt that thing, that indefinable tug she'd been feeling since he touched her on the riverbank. He knew what she knew; that this was no time to pursue whatever it was dangling in front of them. Not for either of them. "We both have big jobs to do at the moment."

"My ten tons haven't fallen around my ankles yet, but they could." Now he could hold her gaze again. "Becoming fire chief means a lot to me. I need to make it work, Melba. For a whole bunch of reasons." The charmer's smile curled up one corner of his mouth. "It's not that I…"

"But…" She didn't let him finish. Clark didn't have anything other than simple friendship to offer her at the moment. And that was best, because neither did she.

Her heart was in tatters for more reasons than just Dad's illness. Her father's secret had just pulled the rug out from underneath everything she knew about love, marriage and family. She'd been so sure Mom and Dad loved each other, but did they really? If her parents were capable of deception and infidelity, what hope did anyone have for a true marriage? The two people Melba trusted most in the world had been keeping huge secrets from her for her whole life. It made her wonder if she'd ever trust anyone again.

No, Melba found herself glad Clark was shutting the door on anything romantic right now. He didn't have the time for it and she…she just didn't have the heart for it. Not now.

Chapter Seven

He should feel better.

Clark had just kept a promise to himself not to let romantic distractions get in the way, even though large parts of him wanted to end that evening in something more than friendship. Melba Wingate was a distraction package wrapped in temptation and tied up with allure. She was completely different from women who usually caught his attention, which made the whole thing even more confounding.

Shaking his head, Clark tried to put her enormous brown eyes out of his mind as he slid his key into the fire station office door…only to find it open. Great. That could only mean one thing. He ducked his head back out the door to eye the station's kitchen window. The bright lights confirmed what he already knew, and the satisfying meal in his stomach turned to stone. For a brief moment, he considered forgetting the files he needed for tomorrow's early morning meeting, but it wasn't any use. Pop would come find him sooner or later. He gritted his teeth as he flipped on the office lights. A bolt of defiance kept him from walking into the kitchen where he knew Pop was waiting. *Let him come to me if he wants to get into this.*

Sure enough, not five minutes later he heard footsteps and looked up from his files to see his father looming cross-armed in the doorway. "You bought Max Jones's boat."

Some days the small-town gossip was more dangerous than half of Detroit's crime syndicates. "I did."

Pop didn't elaborate on his opinion of the purchase, but then he didn't have to—his scowl spoke for him. Clark took a breath to defend the perfectly reasonable desire to own a boat when one lived on a river, but his father cut him off.

"A boat you didn't even own yet before you made a scene on the riverbank with Mort Wingate." He said it with the tone a father would use to scold a young boy for letting a baseball go through the neighbor's window.

Clark felt the itch of a fight climb up his spine. "That was none of my doing."

"Because it's *nothing* like you to open up the motor of your brand-new toy and speed without thinking of the consequences. Churn up enough wake to get an old man wet while he sat on the riverbank."

It was so far from the truth of what happened that Clark didn't know where to start. He stood up, leveraging the six inches he had over his father as a grown man. "Are you even going to bother asking me what really happened?"

Pop's neck began to take on the angry red flush Clark knew too well. "Maybe a better question to ask is why you took Melba Wingate to dinner? Making amends, perhaps? That used to be one of your favorite tactics."

Clark knew he'd be dealing with harsh judgment

when he first moved back into town, but this? After the stand he'd forced himself to take tonight? What was the point of trying for integrity when everyone questioned your motives? He grabbed his file and started for the door. "You are so far out of line, Pop, I don't think it's even worth the effort."

"I wonder what you do find worth the effort?"

That was ironic, considering the effort Clark had put in tonight. It had taken sizable effort to put his interest in Melba Wingate aside and stay focused on what he'd come to town to achieve. He stopped, his head down and his hand on the doorknob. He'd taken the job in Gordon Falls to solve this problem between him and his father, not extend it. *Help me, Lord, I want to wring his neck right now, not be reasonable.* "Pop," he said as calmly as he could manage, "do you have *any* interest in hearing my side of this?"

That caught his father's attention. During the hours of conversations that led up to Clark's nomination as GFVFD's next chief, the one thing each of them had to promise was to hear each other out. They were terrible at it, as tonight displayed. Pop took off his baseball cap, smoothed what was left of his once-red hair and replaced the cap. George Bradens's body language for "I'm changing gears." "Yes," he huffed reluctantly.

"Okay." Clark took his hand off the doorknob. This, of course, meant that when he was done, he'd have to hear out his father's side—which seemed unreasonable at the moment—but there didn't seem to be another way forward. They were going to have to learn to deal with each other. The Bradens clan was down to two; each other was all they had left. If anything happened where he'd need to show his father the kind of patience

Melba showed hers, some large-scale healing was going to need to take place. Might as well start here.

"Want a root beer?" Pop always did his peacekeeping with root beer. There were worse strategies.

"Sure."

Clark tossed the files down on his desk and they walked into the firehouse kitchen. He'd spent so much time in this room it felt more like home than the kitchen at the house. Well, at *Pop's* house—Clark had taken a condo down on the river in the full knowledge that both Bradenses in the same household would spell disaster.

After popping the tops off the bottles, Pop sighed and set them down on the table. "So, you bought a boat," he said with less edge as he eased himself wearily into a chair.

"I'm twenty-eight," Clark said. "I don't need a note from my father." *Okay, Clark,* he reminded himself, *cut out the jabs.* "Yes," he revised, "I bought Jones's boat. A fine boat at a good price. I'm of the mind that I'll need a place to get away from the job stress now and then."

Pop grunted. Whether or not a chief ever truly left work was a point of contention between them. Pop never stopped working, even when he was "off duty." It was one of the reasons skipping out on Melba that first night stuck in Clark's craw so fiercely—he'd been on the receiving end of too many such skips growing up. A host of school baseball games with no Pop in the stands. Too many birthday parties where Pop showed up late—if he showed up at all. And he wasn't the only one who had been neglected. He remembered putting a pillow over his head to block out late-night "don't let Clark hear you!" yelling downstairs in the kitchen when another dinner had gone cold and uneaten.

"And roaring down the river?" Pop made it sound like Clark had spun his tires out on the church front lawn.

Clark pulled his hands down his face—something he'd done way too much of tonight. "Honestly, I'm not sure what happened there. One minute I'm *gently* opening up the throttle under the bridge, the next Mort Wingate is standing knee-deep in the Gordon River yelling at me while his daughter fights to get him to back out."

"'No wake' means just that," his father quoted the buoy marker limiting motorboats to low speeds for that section of the river. He knew Clark well enough to guess "gently opening up the throttle" meant putting on more than a little speed.

And he was right. "Okay, so I was going a bit fast. There wasn't another boat in sight and I didn't see anyone on the bank. It's *April,* for goodness' sake." His dad raised a dubious red-silver eyebrow. "Maybe I should have slowed down, only it wasn't about that. Pop, Mort was yelling at me for scaring away the ducks. Ducks? I could have scared away ducks in a canoe. And even if I did, it hardly rated him wading into the water making a scene like he did. It was…" He stopped short of using the word "crazy." That felt like a low blow to someone battling Alzheimer's.

"You came up on shore." The bank where Mort stood wasn't a legal boat landing. Clark had broken a rule. Or two.

"I came over to help. The guy was three feet into forty-degree water. Melba was frantic trying to pull him out before he fell in all the way." Clark took a swig of the creamy soda. Remembering the wild look in Mort's eyes sent a chill down his back. "It looked like he was coming straight for me, Dad. I figured the best thing to do was to be on land so he came toward dry ground. Melba couldn't control him." It felt lousy to chronicle an old man's weakness, but Clark had to make his dad see the mayhem of the episode. "I didn't have a lot of time to ponder sensible alternatives."

Pop leaned back in his chair, running two fingers along the outside of the root beer bottle. "I could debate whether what happened was your fault—you shouldn't have been going that fast and I don't see why you needed to have *that* boat *right now*—but I'll let that go for now. Still, you expect me to believe you had no sensible alternatives to dinner?"

Now we're getting into it, Clark thought sourly. "You're monitoring my dinner companions now?"

"People talk. That's not news to you."

Clark could have shot down his father's words if his dinner with Melba had been a strictly platonic affair. The truth that his imagination had already wandered too far in regard to Melba—and that he'd only barely managed to rein it back—weakened his defense. How was it Pop managed to make him feel guilty when he hadn't done anything wrong? "I can have dinner with anyone I choose." Clark hated how petulant it sounded.

"Can you?"

Oh, that tone. Pop was a master of the mean-everything-and-say-nothing tone. Nothing got under Clark's skin faster. "Just what is that supposed to mean?"

"Do you need me to spell it out for you, son?"

Clark pushed up off his chair to pace the kitchen.

"Sure. Spell it out for me, Pop. I'm only twenty-eight, surely I can't know what I'm doing here."

"You did not leave Gordon Falls with the best reputation. Small towns have long memories for stuff like that."

"Don't I know it."

"I believe," his father shot back sharply, "that you are capable of stepping in here. I'd never have recommended you for the chief position if I thought you weren't. But it's not all downhill from here and you know it."

"I'm going to have to prove myself." Clark was so sick of hearing that sentence from his father.

"More than prove yourself."

"Because you cast such a long shadow. And everybody loves George Bradens. Nobody can do the job like George does. You know, I'm tired of going over this. And over it and over it." Clark squared off at his father, his temper ignited by Pop's judgmental glare. "I'm *not you.* And as far as the position of fire chief is concerned? I don't want to be. I'm going to give my all to this job but it is not going to eat me alive and become my life. If that's what you or the people in this town expect, then you're all in for a disappointment."

There was a long, prickly silence. "So that's what you think of my dedication, is it?" His father had a long fuse, but there was a massive powder keg at its end.

"No." *Yes. Maybe.* "You know something, Dad? Would you believe I actually put the brakes on things going beyond friendship between Melba and me tonight? Would it even occur to you that I might have told her I needed to keep my focus on the department right now? Or don't you believe I'm capable of that?"

"You were certainly leaning in close enough to have the conversation."

Clark threw his hands up in disgust. "Does no one in Gordon Falls have anything better to do with their time than spy on me? For crying out loud, I can't even seem to do the right thing *when I'm doing the right thing.*"

"The right thing here is to steer clear of Melba Wingate. And Mort, for that matter."

"Were you even listening to what I just said?"

Pop jabbed a finger at him. "And I'm saying that no good can come from you cozying up to the Wingates." He shook his head, readjusting his hat in an angry fluster.

Clark balked. "What is this, the Hatfields and McCoys or something?" There was a look in his father's eye. A flash of something deeper than anger over public perception. "What have you got against the Wingates, anyway?"

"Leave it, Clark."

There was something there, Clark just wasn't sure what it was. "Pop…"

With a practiced aim, Dad shot the empty bottle into the barrel in the corner of the kitchen. "Leave it." His words left no doubt there wasn't even an inch of fuse left before the powder keg blew.

Clark knew enough to leave it. For now.

Melba pulled the door shut on her father's bedroom and exhaled. Her mind shot back to all the times during her childhood when he'd whispered, "Goodnight, Melbadoll," and closed her door. Now she was the one checking on him. Life had gone so topsy-turvy.

Padding down the hall, Melba hit the speed-dial key for Charlotte on her cell phone.

"Hey, I was hoping you'd call." The rhythmic hitch in Charlotte's voice let Melba know she was on the treadmill. The realization made her fall back onto her bed and moan. "How on earth do you have enough energy to be on a treadmill?"

"It's an hour's train ride back to Chicago. That's a lot of sitting for the amount of pie you and I put down during my visit. Besides—" Melba heard her switch off the device "—I didn't spend the afternoon fishing my father out of the Gordon River."

"No, you *helped* me fish my father out of the river." Melba had a hard time even believing the world had handed her reasons to say something so absurd.

"I sent up prayers for you the whole ride home," Charlotte said. "How are things?"

"It's crazy, Charlotte. Barney came and made Dad dinner and he acted like nothing had happened. We all sat in the kitchen while the dryer dried his clothes and pretended the whole episode didn't exist. I feel like I'm in something from *Alice in Wonderland*."

"Does he remember what he did?"

"Who knows?" That was the most frustrating part of all. "He won't discuss it. How am I supposed to go around pretending things are normal when they're absolutely not?"

Charlotte gave a sympathetic sigh. "One of Grandpa's doctors said something to me that stuck. It helped."

"I'll take anything that helps at this point." Melba pulled off a still-damp sock. In all her rush to help Dad, she'd neglected to see to her own soggy feet.

"He said, 'He can't meet you where you are. You

have to meet him where he is.' Your Dad's world has become different than the one we all live in. You have to go visit him there. It's sad, I know, but it makes a kind of sense, doesn't it?"

The truth only seemed to chronicle Dad's now-constant slip from her life. "A sad sense." Charlotte was right; this was a one-way trip. "Oh, Char, every moment feels like it's slipping away forever. I don't know if I can stand by and watch this." She stood up and tossed her socks resolutely into the hamper, determined to have at least one conversation with Charlotte that didn't end with crying.

"Don't stand by. Participate. Go visit him in his world for as long as you can instead of dragging him into yours. It's all you can do, Melba. It's all any of us can do." She heard Charlotte's voice catch at the end, and an even stronger sense came to her of the loss that waited for her at the end of this journey. "Besides—" Charlotte's voice brightened, and Melba could see the blonde shake off her tears as easily as if Charlotte were in the room with her "—you've got handsome Mr. Fire-man to offer some distraction. Wow. I don't usually go for gingers but he could change my mind. Are there more like him at the firehouse?"

"Clark Bradens has made it clear he's not on the market."

"Could have fooled me," Charlotte cooed. "The way he was looking at you? Definitely interested."

"I'm not interested."

"Oh, yes, you are. And if you're not, you should be. I heard him say he goes to your church. All that heroic rescue vibe *and* church? What red-blooded American female wouldn't be interested? Come on, what happened at dinner? I waited a whole ten minutes before asking."

Melba leaned back against the wall, the strength of Clark's gaze heating her memory. "Worst of both worlds. He was really nice and downright charming until…"

Charlotte practically squeaked "Until what?"

"Until he explained that he needs to keep his mind on his job for a while."

"That's too bad."

"No, that's good. I don't need that kind of complication right now."

If a dramatically flung arm had a sound, it was Charlotte's "You're wrong. That's exactly the kind of complication you need."

"Charlotte…"

"So what's next?"

"Dad has a doctor's appointment tomorrow."

"No, I meant with Clark."

Melba put her hand to her forehead. "Weren't you listening? The whole 'his focus is elsewhere' concept? I told you he had a bad reputation when he was younger. Bad boy, troublemaker, womanizer…take your pick. Not everyone's ready to admit he's changed. He's about to take over as fire chief and lots of people aren't happy about it. Proving himself in that role is his focus for now. And that's *good*."

"Well, Clark or no Clark, you've still got to make new friends. I can't come out there and save you every time—you need local backup. Someone a little younger than Grandma Barney. When does that women's group meet at the church?"

"Tomorrow afternoon."

"Good. I'll expect an email Wednesday morning with a list of all your new small-town friends. Tell me how many are in the group and I'll scour up all those extra prayer-shawl kits from last quarter's catalogue promotion."

"I have no idea if any of them knit, Charlotte."

"Who cares if none of them do...yet? You can teach them. What better way to make friends?"

Melba stared at her knitting bag, letting the warm memory of sitting in the living room stitching with Charlotte remind her how much it soothed her. How she'd never have made it through the hours of doctor and hospital visits without yarn and needles. How lovely it would be to have something in her world that didn't revolve around Dad and medicine. "I hate it when you're right all the time."

Charlotte laughed. "Nonsense. It's why you love me."

"I do, you know. You've been great. Thanks for coming out...and for everything." Melba felt her voice catch again, suddenly exhausted from the long, dramatic day.

"I'm praying for you. Every day. I know you can make it. And you know what will happen if I don't have an email in my box by noon on Wednesday."

Melba hung up the phone with a sigh. She did need some new friends. Only trouble was, the best candidate for the job made her think about a lot more than friendship. Clark was warm and supportive, but he was also handsome and wildly charismatic—way too much for her tender heart to handle right now. Charlotte was right; the women's group was exactly where she needed to be. *Just one good woman friend nearby, Lord. That's all I need.*

Chapter Eight

"I'd be happy to come visit with Mort to free you up
for the women's group."

Melba stared at Pastor Allen. "You'd do that for me?"

A wry smile curled the edges of his mouth in the
friendliest of ways. "Who says I'm doing it for you? I
like spending time with your dad."

"Really?" Melba's reaction pinched her own heart.
When had spending time with Dad become more obli-
gation than pleasure? It stung to know some part of her
thought it a chore to be around him now. "Of course,"
she shot back with too much enthusiasm. "Dad's a nice
guy to be around." She didn't think she covered her
gaffe well.

"Even nice guys are hard to take nonstop." So he
had noticed. Melba felt shame flush her cheeks. "And
Barney tells me your dad can be a bit of a handful
these days."

She fished for the right response, but came up empty.
All of her brave endurance eluded her this morning.
When Barney pushed Melba into Pastor Allen's office
and then took Dad down the hall to the church parlor

for a cup of coffee, she'd felt like she was begging for scraps of help she didn't want to admit she needed. Allen put a hand on her shoulder, and the ever-present lump in her throat tightened its grip again.

"The women's group loves new members, especially ones who come with such great new ideas. I'd never even heard of a prayer shawl ministry until Barney mentioned it. I'd love for you to get one going here. Abby Reed is in the group, and she owns the local craft shop. She'll be all over this in a heartbeat. I'm eager to get you connected into the community." He paused for a moment before adding, "I think you'll need it." Allen gestured toward the hallway. "Barney will take today, and I'll be Mort's buddy for the rest of the meetings. Consider me his standing coffee date for every other Tuesday afternoon. Is that all right with you?"

While she'd seen a few of them around the church, and remembered others from years and years ago, Melba felt like she didn't really know any of the women in that group. Still, her spirit felt instantly lighter. At least for ninety minutes every other week, Melba had somewhere to go, something to do that didn't involve Dad's constant care. "It's marvelous. Thank you so much."

"It's what I do. It's what we all do. Let's go get you introduced."

It wasn't hard to guess which room held the Tuesday Women. She heard the boisterous chatter from halfway down the hall. Just before she turned the corner into the room, the women broke out in uproarious laughter so that Melba walked into a wave of guffaws.

"He didn't!" an older woman Melba vaguely recognized wheezed as she wiped her tearing eyes.

"I told him to check for those red socks, that sorting

is an essential part of laundry, but would he listen? Not a bit. Serves him right." A woman with curly blond hair was trying to sound serious behind mischievous eyes.

"Abby," said the older woman, "tell me you bought the boy new ones."

The woman Melba realized was Abby Reed crossed her arms. "I did not. I told him if he wasn't going to take my advice, then he could march his own money down to Halverson's and buy his own undershirts and socks." Abby's declaration sent the women into further giggles until Melba was nearly laughing herself.

"Melba," cut in Pastor Allen, "This is Abby Reed. To her left is Marge Bowers—I think she taught you in Sunday school—then Tina Matthews. And you may remember Violet Sharpton who's next to her." He pointed to the older woman who waved cheerfully even though still wiping her eyes. "And whether or not you remember Jeannie Owens, you should make sure you stop by her new candy shop on the way home."

"Abby's boy Ben just failed his first laundry lesson," Violet piped up. "With flying colors."

"Or should I say running colors," Abby added. "You'll know my son by his new wardrobe of pink T-shirts."

"I think this is exactly where I should leave," Pastor Allen said. "Ladies, if you don't know, this is Mort Wingate's daughter, Melba. You all take good care of her. She's got a special project for all of you, too."

Melba tried to place Jeannie Owens and the candy shop in her memory as the woman scooted over on the couch. "There's a spot for you right here. How's your dad? I heard you had a bit of an…episode…over the weekend but he's okay?"

Melba's embarrassment must have been clear on her face because Marge gave a derisive snort and said, "Yep, everybody knows everything around here. Everybody knows too much, if you ask me." She reached out and patted Melba's hand. "I do remember you from Sunday school. You ought to know something like that gets around town faster than floodwaters. Don't you worry about that, though, we'll back you up. This here is a formidable group, and you're one of us now."

The whole group nodded, squaring their shoulders like they were ready to take on any comers, and Melba felt herself smile. "That fast?"

"That fast." Violet Sharpton grasped Melba's hand with a startlingly firm grip. "For us, at least. Some of the other old biddies, they take a while to come around. But us? We know good people when we see them." Violet's high cheekbones framed a smile as warm as her hands were strong. "And some of us have lived long enough to know when a gal could use a friend or two. Or five." She gave Melba's hand a reassuring shake.

Tina slid a mug across the coffee table until it sat in front of Melba. "Vi's husband hung on six long years after his stroke. She knows a thing or two about taking care of someone. Barney helped her out in Edward's final days, too. You've got a lot in common. Cream or sugar?"

"Oh," Melba replied sheepishly, "I'm a tea person myself."

"Finally!" Violet threw her hands up in the air. "Someone else in this room who grasps the elegance of something besides coffee." She winked one clear gray eye at Melba. "We'll get along marvelously."

Abby laughed. "Violet, I have yet to meet the person you don't immediately adore."

Violet's eyes narrowed. "I'll tell you, I don't much care for that new grocery bagger down at Milton's. Looks at me funny. Like I remind him of some long-lost love or something."

That made Abby laugh harder. "That one with the brown curly hair? He's all of seventeen. You'd be more like his long-lost granny."

Violet straightened and ran a hand through her beautifully cut silver hair. "I was a stunner in my day, I'll have you know. I still have to fight them off at the senior fish fry."

This sent the whole circle into a fit of laughter. The joyful sound washed over Melba like a wave of peace. No one here was her age—in fact the women here were a collection of every age but hers—and yet she felt blissfully welcome, instantly at ease. It had been so long since she'd made a new friend that she'd forgotten how delightful it could be.

The six of them chatted for half an hour about small, ordinary topics. Undramatic, ordinary things that helped Melba remember a time would come where every day didn't hold a new trauma. Tina finally picked up the book each of them had and waved it in their faces. "I see we're not going to get to chapter three today, so let's just drop our agenda for the afternoon and take it up next time."

"I figured we dropped the agenda twenty minutes ago." Violet gave Melba a knowing glance. "Tina has to declare everything."

Tina, a hefty woman with a full face framed with thick black hair, fisted her hands on her ample hips.

"That's because someone has to keep you all in line or we'd never get anything accomplished."

"Speaking of accomplishments," Abby cut in with a sugary let's-not-get-into-that voice, "Pastor Allen said something about a project? This group *needs* a project. I want to hear what you've got in mind."

Clark hoped that once he was officially fire chief, tasks like arts and crafts would be off his agenda. He'd heard of departments that had women's auxiliaries, and surely any female would be in a better position than he to be standing in the fabric aisle of Abby Reed's Creative Pursuits store buying forty 12x12-inch squares of red flannel. What was bric-a-brac, anyway?

In the unavoidable impulse of all firemen, Clark found himself assessing how quickly all the store's contents—fluffy quilt batting, a million kinds of yarn and far too many acres of scrapbook paper—would go up in flames. How many times had Clark entered a large public space and had his first response not be to enjoy the architecture or decor, but to scan the ceiling and count sprinkler heads? How many times had he watched his father's head turn towards the exits or tilt up toward the ceilings upon entering any building? Pop was right about one thing: a fireman wasn't about what you did, it was about who you were. Parts of the role never came off, even when the uniform was long retired.

"You look a little lost. Can I help you find something?"

Clark turned to find a perky young woman in the store's trademark pink aprons standing next to him. Deciding that the silly-sounding question might get him out of the store faster, he ventured, "What on earth is bric-a-brac and where can I find it?"

She laughed at his obvious disdain. "It's over here with the ribbons and trimmings." Spying the crumpled sheet, she nodded toward it. He noticed her name tag said "Libby" in bright pink letters. "Some kind of school project?"

He gladly handed the paper over. "Fireman Friendly Awareness Day is next week."

Recognition played across her young, round face. About seventeen by Clark's guess, she looked exactly like someone named Libby ought to look. "Hey, you're Clark Bradens, aren't you?" Her smile broadened. "You're gonna be chief, right? Oh, these are so adorable!" Her voice pitched up in that high-school squeal—how had he found that attractive ten years ago when it grated like fingernails on a chalkboard now?

"You used to love puzzles, didn't you, Dad?" came a familiar voice a few aisles away. Deep and velvety, full of warmth but a bit weary. Melba. The contradiction in the voices—and the effect each had on him—startled Clark. He wanted to peer around the aisle and see her, not follow the grinning high school girl heading toward the ribbon aisle.

"Dr. Nichols said puzzles would be good for you."

"I don't remember him saying anything of the sort." Mort sounded like a two-year-old being presented with creamed spinach.

"Well, let's just see if we can pick one or two that you might like. We can do them together." Melba's voice had the kind-hearted parental quality he'd seen her use with her father before. His conscience pricked him hard.

When was the last time you showed that much grace to your own father?

Following Libby, Clark slowed at the end of the aisle, looking in the direction of Melba's voice. She looked up just in time to see him. The reaction on her face was a pleasant, careful surprise—a silent "Hi there!" as she nodded toward her father currently crouched over to peer at puzzle boxes. She managed a small wave, and he felt the flutter of her fingers somewhere deep under his ribs. Melba had the kind of eyes that hardly needed the addition of speech—they were infinitely expressive, saying far more than her words ever did. At least to him. The old expression "windows to the soul" made sense when he looked at her.

"Over here, Chief!" Libby squeaked, now two aisles away.

Chief. It was the first time anyone had called Clark "Chief," and it jolted him out of his Melba-induced stupor. Chief Bradens. In a few weeks' time, that wouldn't mean his father, but him. Swallowing a sigh, Clark had to wonder if God hadn't just sent the exact thought to shake him back to his senses. *No distractions.*

Managing a foolish shrug of his shoulders, Clark nodded toward Libby's call of "Did you get lost, Chief?" and dragged himself over to the ribbons aisle.

"Here's what you need, right here." The bubbly clerk hoisted a spool of black squiggly ribbon matching the illustration on his supply sheet. She twisted it so he could see the label. "Bric-a-brac. You know, I don't know why they call it that." Her high-pitched giggle made Clark feel a million years old. "Something to look up when I get online tonight, I suppose."

"Yeah." Clark lingered at the end of the aisle where,

if he leaned just right, he could peer back to the puzzle section.

"How much do you need?"

Melba's face, that delightful tumble of brown curls falling around it, appeared around the corner. He was unable to stop himself from smiling, even though she pulled quickly back when she realized Clark caught her peeking. He was peeking himself, wasn't he?

Libby tapped his shoulder with the spool of ribbon. "How much does the paper say you need?"

"Um…"

With an amused sigh, she pulled the paper from Clark's hand. "Wow. They really sent the wrong guy, didn't they?"

Boy, do we need a Ladies Auxiliary was Clark's thought, sure there was no "right" fireman to send for sewing notions. "I suppose so." He thought he heard a chuckle from the puzzle section. A decidedly female, decidedly familiar laugh that tickled warm down the back of his neck. He used his height to peer over the shelves, catching sight of the top of her hair as she moved away from him. He had the sudden craving to peek again, to catch Melba's eyes in a quick, secretive glance and feel that jolt in the pit of his stomach one more time.

"'Two feet per student,'" read Libby. "How many students are you buying for?"

Clark dragged his thoughts back to the task at hand. "Forty kids."

She scrunched up her pale eyebrows in calculation. "Two feet times forty kids is eighty feet, divided by three for yardage is…"

He waited, thinking it rude to beat her to the number

when this was her job. When the pause became unbearable, he piped up, "A little bit over twenty seven yards."

"Handsome and smart. Maybe they *did* send the right guy." She actually winked at him, and Clark did not know what to do with that. "Of course, the whole roll is thirty yards, and you get twenty percent off if you buy the whole roll, so you're better off doing that. Extra for mistakes and all." She popped the large spool of black ribbon into Clark's basket with a flourish of salesmanship pride. "Anything else?"

For a rebellious second, Clark thought about declaring the need for a puzzle. Then he remembered his last encounter with Mort, and came to his senses. "No, that's everything."

"Well then, Chief, let's get you checked out and back to the station." Libby was obviously having loads of fun with the concept of waiting on the fire chief, even if it made Clark inwardly cringe. There was a time when he would have relished this kind of adoration. Even now he could practically feel his father rolling his eyes in contempt.

The path to the cash register took him past where Melba stood with her father. Although he told himself repeatedly not to do it, he slowed his steps and glanced up toward her. She was looking straight at him, as if she'd been watching for him to pass by. In the seconds they held each other's gaze, he collected a dozen details. The way her fingers played with the rings on her right hand. The way a spiraling lock of that distracting hair always hung over one eye. How the blue color of her scarf made her eyes stand out even more. The way she opened her mouth to say something until he held a "shh" finger to his lips. The playful "don't tell" gesture came out of nowhere, from some place inside he couldn't seem to successfully tamp down around her despite his brain's shouts of "What are you doing?"

He wished he knew the answer.

Chapter Nine

"See, Mort? You'll have a grand time doing these. Are you sure you don't want a third one? Smart guy like you will go through these too fast, if you ask me." Abby Reed was coddling Dad so enthusiastically that Melba wondered if she'd let too much of her stress show in the women's group earlier.

"I was thinking the same thing," Mort said, beaming at the compliment. "That really intricate one looked like it would pose a good challenge." The pride in his voice made Melba ashamed that she'd steered him away from the difficult puzzle. He was a smart man—was still a smart man in many ways. It was wrong of her to act as if memory loss made him less intelligent.

"Well, mosey on back there and pick it out while I chat with Melba a bit about a project."

Mort narrowed his eyes. "A project? You and Melba?"

"She's going to teach our women's group to knit. Well, some of us. Tina already knows how, and she'll probably lord it over the rest of us. We're going to make prayer shawls."

"What?"

"Prayer shawls, Dad. Like the kind I made back at my church in the city. You knit them, say prayers over them, and give them to people who need comfort. I made you one last year."

Mort pinched the bridge of his nose, thinking hard. Melba found herself holding her breath, praying for his memory to function for just this tiny fact. She needed to see him remember something. Dad turned and looked at her. "That green thing with the fringe on the end?"

"Yes, that's it." She hoped the desperate relief she felt didn't show in her voice. Abby caught her eye for a split second, recognizing Melba's stress but not pointing it out to Mort in any way.

"I like that thing. Very comfortable. Warm." His pronouncement made, he waved them off as he started back toward the puzzle aisle. "Sounds like a good way to keep her busy to me," he called over his shoulder.

Melba could only chuckle and shake her head while Abby put her hand on her chest and looked at Mort with a sadly sweet smile. "He's a grand guy, your pop. I've known him since I was a teenager. My first job was cleaning rooms at your folks' resort—only back then I was Abby Morris and my hair was...well, let's just say it wasn't quite this color."

"I remember...sort of."

"I was sorry to see it shut down, but it was too much for your dad to handle alone after your mom passed." Abby's eyes shifted back to Melba. "She was a neat lady. I've always liked your folks." She settled herself into a more cheerful expression. "And now I get to like you, too. Although I'm skeptical—you're not the first person to try to teach me to knit. I'll warn you previous efforts have not met with success."

"Let's just say Dad and I could both use a challenge these days." It was odd, but Melba could feel herself settling into the community bit by bit. Some conversations—like this one—bloomed a nearly physical sensation in her chest. The slow grounding of renewed connections, a tree spreading roots like children spread their toes in the sand. "Can you pull up my company's website from here?"

Abby tilted the computer screen so they both could see, and Melba guided her to the portion of the company catalogue that featured soft, plush yarns and the free downloadable patterns for prayer shawls. In no time at all, she and Abby had sent an email to Charlotte telling her how many kits they would need to provide yarn and supplies for the entire group.

"So," Abby said, her tone changing entirely as she nodded to the other side of the store, "about that over there."

"About what?"

"Those looks. Clark Bradens peering at you every chance he got."

Melba coached herself not to look surprised or to show even the slightest hint that she got what Abby was talking about. "Clark said hello."

Abby leaned over the cash register and lowered her voice. "Sure, he said hello, but that man's eyes said a whole lot more."

Do not flush, do not flush, Melba commanded herself as she waved away the comment. "Don't be ridiculous. If he was checking on me, it's just because he knows how rough things have been. He helped me with Dad the other day when things got…difficult."

"Clocks or mountains?" Dad hollered from the puzzle aisle as if he'd heard Abby's whisper of his name.

Melba put her hand to her forehead, unable to take assaults from two fronts at once. "Um…how about mountains?" Perhaps the exchange would put a stop to Abby's direction of conversation.

It didn't. "Word is he also helped you with dinner that night. That's above and beyond my definition of rescue." When Melba glared at her, Abby threw her hands up in defense. "Small towns have big eyes and big ears."

"And *bigger mouths*," she shot back. Was having everyone sticking their nose in her business the price she paid for a tight-knit community? It didn't seem like much of a fair trade at the moment.

"Gossip is one thing," Abby conceded. "But the way that man peered around my aisles was another."

It was obvious. She had to grant Abby that. "He's been nice to me."

"It's a nice thing to have a nice man be nice to you. I'm all for it." Abby winked. "Just in case you're looking for someone to back you up."

In this case, "back you up" was starting to look far too much like "match you up," and that was the last thing Melba could handle right now. "Abby—" Melba looked her straight in the eyes, trying to send the clearest possible message "—whatever you saw, thought you saw or wished you'd seen, this really isn't the time." It was the truth.

"Clocks it is," Dad called loudly.

"*Really* not the time," Melba emphasized. At almost the same moment, the two women realized the "clocks"-

"time" ironic connection, and began to laugh. It broke the mild tension of the moment, and set Melba at ease again. She cleared her throat and squared her shoulders, hoping to broadcast the end of that conversational topic. "The kits don't have needles. Have you got enough for everyone?"

Abby gave her one long, woeful look, then reached behind her for a notebook and flipped it open. "Let's check. You said size eleven or thirteen, right?"

"Those are best. And we'll only need four, since Tina and I already have our own." The store had the appropriate needles in stock, so everything was in place by the time Dad sauntered back with a puzzle depicting an intricate pen-and-ink drawing of several clocks.

"Clocks." He placed it on the table with pride, pointing to the label in one corner that said "Challenging: 2000 pieces."

"Loads of 'em. And no colors to cheat by." Abby sounded genuinely impressed at the black-and-white illustration. "That takes confidence."

"Order in a few more," Mort said, pushing the box across the counter to her. "You've got nothing else up at my level." There, right in front of her, was the old Mort Wingate. Wearing the same stubborn expression that allowed him to tackle the thousand endless problems of running a resort for thirty years. Mama always said he chewed at a problem like a dog at a bone—relentless until he managed a solution. Every time Melba sank into despair that her father was disappearing right in front of her eyes, he'd reappear as his old self, strong and solid.

On the one hand, the shows of strength were treasures, footholds in the fog. On the other hand, they made the weaker episodes much harder to bear. "Oh, by the way," Mort said with a twinkle in his eye, "if it's all the same to you, I'll take this hard one up to church the next time we go. It'll give Pastor Allen and me something to do until fishing season. That man don't know much about fishing if he thinks anything's biting this early in the year."

Melba could only smile. "It's just fine by me." She glanced at the clocks and thought something celebrating the passing of time wasn't the kind of thing she wanted to spend hours staring at these days. Time felt too much like her enemy. "Looks over my head anyway."

Mort gave a grunt. "Nonsense. You're smart."

Melba imitated his derisive noise. "You're smarter." *You were,* she thought silently. *You still are in lots of ways, if I can only try to remember that.*

"I can't see how this is going to comfort anyone." Marge frowned at the inch of knitting she'd wrestled into being over the last half hour. "I thought it was a nice subtle color but now I think it just looks like seaweed."

This part of the yarn—for Melba knew it changed colors gradually—did have an unfortunately murky green hue. Marge's first attempt at knitting wasn't helping the metaphor, filled with knots and holes as it was. During their last session, Abby had brought over an enormous basket with the kits Charlotte had shipped and let everyone pick their colors. It had made Melba smile to watch, for she could tell so much about each woman by the color they chose. Between that and the first lesson on how to knit, she'd already felt strong friendships growing with each of them. If that had ever happened so fast at any of her city knitting nights, she couldn't remember it.

"What's wrong with that? Botanical is very 'in' this season," Abby remarked from over her sky-blue swath of stitches. "And besides, we live on a river. We don't get seaweed, that's an ocean thing."

Marge poked her finger through one of the larger holes. "Well, then it looks like something that washed up out of the river."

Tina left her stitching to reach over and touch the green inch. "It's very soft. You don't often get that kind of fluffy quality in a machine-washable yarn. I bet your company sells a lot of this yarn, Melba."

"It's one of our bestselling products. Even before so many people made prayer shawls with it." It was so delightful to be talking about fiber and knitting again. Not only because she loved those things, but because it had felt like that part of her life had been cut off until now. Talking textiles made Melba feel like Melba again, not just Mort's scrambling caregiver. Had Pastor Allen offered to keep Dad company because he recognized how badly she needed this time? Or was that just God's grace showing up where she least expected it?

"Oh, I almost forgot." Violet put down her bright pink yarn. It hadn't surprised Melba a bit that Violet had chosen a near-neon pink or that the tiny woman had taken to knitting like a duck to water. She'd come back after the last session with nearly two feet completed. Fishing around in her knitting bag—one from the cover of Melba's employer's latest catalogue—Violet pronounced, "I need a man."

Conversation ground to a halt. Marge's eyebrows shot up nearly to her hairline.

"Good gracious, ladies, I mean I need a man's *head*." Violet laughed, producing a bright red knit hat Melba recognized from one of the free downloadable patterns on the company website. "How on earth do I know what size a college student's head is? I took a look at a photo of Jason holding a basketball and tried to eyeball it, but who knows if I even came close?"

"You made a hat? Already?" Tina's voice held the masked disappointment of a woman whose knitting superiority had just been thrown into serious jeopardy.

"It's just like the shawl, only smaller. When I got to the part where you decrease, I just looked it up on the internet. They had videos and everything."

"You've done a wonderful job," Melba praised, genuinely impressed.

"It's red. Really, really red," Abby offered. "I thought college students didn't go for colors like that."

Violet crinkled her eyes, peering at the little point that made up the top of the hat. "School colors. The other color is white. I thought about trying stripes, but I figured he'd end up looking like a candy cane or that fellow kids look for in books."

This produced a bevy of blank looks until Abby's face lit up. "You mean Waldo? As in *Where's Waldo?* Oh, goodness, with Jason's glasses he *would* look just like Waldo." She giggled. "That would be funny, I admit."

"Not to Jason. He likes to look serious." Violet turned the hat this way and that, inspecting it.

"Serious? He's going to look like an elf," Marge commented. "You'll spot the boy a mile away in that thing."

"The boy is six foot five. He'll hardly look like an elf." She raised an eyebrow. "A white pom-pom?"

The suggestion made Abby Reed burst into laughter.

"Vi," she said, "you do want your grandson to like you when this is over, don't you? No pom-poms. Really."

Melba nodded in agreement, trying to imagine a six-foot-five version of Waldo. "It's fine just the way it is, Violet."

"Fine? It could be huge or too small for all I know. Which is why," Violet said looking around the room, "I need a man."

"What about Pastor Allen?" Tina offered.

"He's out with my dad," Melba answered. "I'd try it on myself, but I don't think that would help you. It looks like the right size." She really wanted to encourage the way Violet had dived into the craft, wanted to give her the thrill of seeing something she made on the head of a man the size of her grandson. A woman's first knitted garment was a memorable achievement—she still had her first scarf, sloppy and lumpy as it was.

Her solution presented itself when Melba spied Clark Bradens walking down the street in the direction of the firehouse. "Ladies," she said, holding up one finger as she jumped out of her chair, "I've got our man."

Dashing down the hall, Melba pushed open the church's side door to yell "Clark!" just as he was about to turn the corner. The megawatt smile that filled his face when he caught sight of her hitched her breath, and she had to remind herself this was for Violet's encouragement, not her enjoyment. She called him over with a wave of her hand. "How tall are you?"

"Six-two. Why?"

"Can I borrow you for a minute?"

Melba never really thought of twinkling eyes as a masculine trait, but Clark's eyes had a way of radiating energy and amusement that could only be called a twinkle. "Can't reach the top shelf?"

She felt her own glow of energy. "Not exactly. You'll be more of a mannequin than a ladder, really."

Clark's furrowed brows and frown were forced, not hiding his amusement one bit. "Oh, I don't think I like the sound of that."

She grabbed his elbow and tugged him in. "I need you for ten seconds to encourage a lovely lady."

Now the twinkle in his eye took on what she remembered as the heart-slaying Clark Bradens gleam. "I'll want more than ten seconds to do that."

Melba laughed, unable to stop the heat from rising up in her chest. How could he look so nice *and* look so able to kiss a woman senseless at the same time? "I'm sure Violet Sharpton will be happy to oblige."

Clark pulled back. "Violet?"

"Long story," Melba said, even though it wasn't. "Here's your chance to get in with the church lady demographic."

"I know I said the 'old biddies' were getting to me, but I wasn't planning a promotional campaign."

She tugged on his arm again, enjoying a sense of playfulness she thought she'd lost completely up until now. "Come on. I need you. Just for a minute."

Chapter Ten

"You know, when the pretty lady said 'I need you,' I saw this going a whole lot differently." Clark tried to find a way to stand so as not to look ridiculous in his current choice of headwear, but it was hopeless. Violet Sharpton had actually climbed on a chair to put the hat on him—something he strongly discouraged to no avail. The old ladies were having far too much fun at his expense. "Mrs. Sharpton, *please* get down."

"Not…just…yet." She adjusted the hat for the sixth time. He was pretty sure she was just messing with him, but she was so small and so adorable—and so very well respected in the church ladies guild—that he rolled his eyes and relented. "There," she said, scanning him with narrowed eyes. "How's it feel?"

He looked sideways at the old woman. He ought to be mad, but somehow he just couldn't summon the irritation. "The hat or my dignity?"

Violet swatted his shoulder. "The hat." Her assessing frown curled into a knowing smile. "And from what I hear, your ego could always stand a ding or two."

The younger Clark—the angry young man with loads

to prove—would have ensured a cutting comeback to a remark like that. Clark wasn't that angry young man anymore. He still had a few things to prove, but none of those prevented him from raising one eyebrow in bemused agreement. Maybe he didn't have to fight his previous reputation so hard, just connect with people the way he was now.

Even managing a begrudging laugh, Clark extended his hand and helped Violet off the chair. Melba caught his eye as he did, something that did not go unnoticed among the giggling circle of church ladies who currently served as his audience. If he were being strategic about the whole thing, he could rationalize that Melba wasn't far off in her assessment that this would give him an "in"; the group before him represented some of the most influential ladies at Gordon Falls Community Church. Only it wasn't some strategy. Clark found himself discovering he actually enjoyed being a nice guy, dropping the hard shell of his tough-guy past. If taking ten minutes of looking like an overgrown elf made him a bit like Pop, maybe that wasn't such a bad thing. "The hat feels wonderful. Warm and cozy."

Abby Reed narrowed her eyes. "It doesn't feel too… what's a word Ben would use…dorky?" Though she pretended to be focused on the hat, he'd caught her glance ricocheting back and forth between himself and Melba. It didn't surprise him. Abby Reed was a notorious matchmaker—she'd taken credit for Jeannie and Chad after all—and Clark suspected even the furniture could pick up on the full-out attraction that hummed between him and Melba. An attraction that he'd resolved to ignore—just the way he'd ignore Abby's assessing looks and would focus on the question she'd actually asked instead.

Of course it felt dorky. It felt beyond dorky, but he wasn't about to say that to Violet Sharpton's jubilant face. "You're asking a firefighter if he likes wearing a red hat? That's like asking a fish if he likes water." *Thanks, Lord,* Clark sent up a silent prayer of gratitude that a suitable dodge to that loaded question had come to mind.

"I'm sure Melba could make you one," Abby cooed. Melba hid behind her curls but he could still see her blushing wildly.

"I'm sure Melba has better things to do with her time," he replied. He mugged at the group and made a slow turn before pulling off the hat. It was a bit tight, but surprisingly comfortable and very warm. He handed the hat back to Violet. "Your grandson will love it. Make him a scarf to match."

Marge Bowers surveyed him from behind her crossed arms in an overstuffed chair. "You'll do just fine, Clark. Do your daddy proud, you will."

"You owe me pie," Clark said, pointing at Melba with mock seriousness as he held open the church exit door. "Maybe even doughnuts."

She grinned. "I owe you nothing. I just handed you the GFCC knitting guild's seal of endorsement."

"You're a guild now, are you?" He pulled the door shut behind them, Melba hugging her elbows against the still-nippy April air. "I suppose I should be happy none of them got out their cell phones to take pictures. Had you done that at the firehouse, I'd have been up on the internet before Violet was down off her chair."

"You were a good sport." Melba laughed, and the sound hummed under his skin. Low and musical, its presence made him realize how much he enjoyed making her smile. Maybe that was because when she first came back to town he'd met her under such sorry circumstances—more than one sorry circumstance, actually. Maybe it was that he could imagine falling for her all too easily. There wasn't another sensible reason why he'd just donned the dumbest-looking hat he'd ever seen and pretended it was no big deal.

"I'll insist you swear Jeannie Owens to secrecy. If Chad ever found out about this, I'd never hear the end of it." Clark sighed, realizing there'd be no way to keep something this gossip-worthy under wraps for long. "I'm probably already sunk." He should have been at P.A. Crimson to talk about those fire hoses twenty minutes ago, but he couldn't bring himself to move off the church steps.

Melba touched his elbow. "It was for a good cause. Violet really is proud of that hat. I've never seen anyone take to knitting so fast and with that kind of enthusiasm. And at her age, even. I really like her. She must have been a firecracker in her youth."

"See?" Clark resisted the urge to place his hand over hers. "You're getting connected already. They adore you in there. They recognize you bring your own gifts, not just taking care of Mort." He allowed himself one good long look into her eyes. "You're stronger than you think, Melba Wingate."

He'd struck a nerve. She looked around—everywhere but at him—while she pulled in a breath and blinked hard. "No, I'm not. I'm a mess at the end of my rope, that's what I am."

He could no longer resist reaching out to her, and she shivered a bit when he touched her shoulder. "But you've already tied a few good knots to hang on to. And God will send more as you need 'em. I know a survivor when I see one, and you're going to do okay. Really." One tear slipped down her cheek, and Clark felt his conviction slide down with it. "Tell you what."

"What?" she sniffed.

"You go back in there and lead the faithful to their stitches, and we'll go out on my boat tomorrow." Was it a smart decision? No. But she needed a friend so badly—and he wanted it to be him. "Barney's at your house all afternoon tomorrow, isn't she?"

"Well, yeah." There it was. That sparkle of hope he could never quite get out of the back of his mind. "I suppose it'd be nice to get away." It only took the tiniest bit of encouragement to pull her back from her dark corners. She seemed so ready to hunt out the good in something—or at least she had been and had forgotten it. Just by watching her face, he could see the woman of extraordinary strength she would be when she came out of this tough time.

"I am a master of the thirty-minute vacation. You could learn a lot from me." He had a picture of her laughing full and loud on the river, the wind tumbling through that incredible hair, sun splashing gold on her face. And he'd be right there with her. As a friend. Just a friend, absolutely and completely nothing more than a friend.

"It sounds wonderful…but…"

"No," he said, daring to put a finger to her lips. That was a mistake. The contact shot through him, giving him twelve incredibly tempting and riotously stupid ideas, all of which should be abandoned immediately. "Don't give me reasons you can't." He hadn't squelched any of those rebellious impulses from his youth, after all. Evidently all they needed was the right inspiration, and it was standing in front of him. "You owe me. The dock behind Jones River Sports tomorrow at one." With an application of willpower that practically made him groan, he stepped back and added, "And don't you dare bring your knitting."

"Okay." He felt the fall of her resistance slide down the back of his neck and settle with warm satisfaction under his ribs. She was so different than anyone who'd ever caught his eye. Years ago this might have been about conquest or the thrill of the chase, but his connection with her went so deep so fast it felt like God was unlocking some part of him he was finally ready to view. But *was* he ready? A week ago, he would have said he definitely wasn't. But now?

Now he wasn't so sure.

Melba could almost convince herself life was normal. She had new friends, she was knitting again, and every moment didn't feel drastic. She and Dad had shared a simple dinner that night, and now they sat in the living room enjoying the close of the day. Melba sat in her mother's chair, working on the midsection of a sample prayer shawl for the knitting group. She'd always felt like a trespasser in this chair, but tonight she felt connected to her mother, grounded in a new and comfortable way. Tonight Melba could feel her influence everywhere in the cozy house, could pull up mental images of Mom touching this object or that, sitting in this chair or staring at that framed photograph. It was as if "home" had finally unfolded to meet her, as if the house opened up its embrace. She felt "settled" for the first time since transplanting her life back to Gordon Falls.

No doubt some of this feeling came from Gordon Falls's newfound appeal. Pastor Allen was right, the women of the knitting group had become instant friends. Yes, they were all older—some by lots and some by only a little—but she welcomed their wisdom and the head-on practicality they showed when facing challenges. Especially Violet. Melba cringed when she remembered how she used to think of "strange Mrs. Sharpton." Now, as she remembered Violet perched on a chair adjusting that outrageous hat on Clark's clashing red hair, she adored the woman.

"You look so like your mother, sitting there."

Melba looked up to see her father staring at her, his jigsaw puzzle abandoned on the coffee table. Despite the wistful look in his eyes, his expression was as clear and lucid as when she was a teenager. The surge of urgency, the desperate desire to grab hold of these clear moments and hoard them before they disappeared forever, almost made her gasp. Instead she placed a casual smile on her face. "That's nice to hear."

"That was her chair. She made the afghan on our bed sitting right there, waiting for you to come home from band practice. Did you know she'd played the flute in high school, too?"

"I'd forgotten." It was delightfully unsettling to have Dad remember something that had slipped her mind. He was still all in there—hidden from view sometimes, but still all there.

"That chair used to be in our nursery." He chuckled, and she tucked away the sound to remember forever.

"You were such a cranky baby, she'd end up rocking you for hours." He shifted in his chair and pointed at her with eyes all squinted up in amusement. "I even found a contraption down at Lindwig's Antiques once, a sort of cradle/chair combination so she could rock you and play her flute or knit. Thought I'd solved her problem, but no. You'd have none of the thing—you wanted your mother's arms and nothing but." A wisp of shadow crossed his eyes for a moment, as if he'd bit into something sour.

"Did you ever rock me?" The question seemed ludicrous and terribly important all at once. As if it would be the key that would unlock the whole dark conversation she both craved and dreaded.

Dad's mouth worked for a moment before he answered. "Now and then, when you'd let me or when Maria was too tired to care what you wanted." He looked like he was going to say more, but fell silent.

"What was she like? Back when you were first married, I mean." She cocked her head to one side and winked at him. "Before I came along in all my crankiness."

"Your mother?" He ran one hand over the white doily covering the chair's arm. Mom had crocheted those, too, only now they were tinted with age and use. "She was a beauty. Fragile in some ways, tough as nails in others." He looked up. "She could melt your heart with those eyes—same big brown ones she gave you." He smiled, a faraway kind of smile as if some memory had just popped up. "One look and she could get anything she wanted out of me. I thought sheep on the resort were the worst idea ever, but she kept staring at me with those big eyes and pretty soon, we had sheep wandering out in back."

Those sheep had given birth to Melba's love of fiber and fiber arts. Another gift of her mother's passed on to her. "Did you know each other in high school?" Melba knew they'd met at the homecoming dance his senior year, but she wanted Dad to tell the story.

"I had eyes for her two years before she ever let me take her out." He reached up and touched his own white-blond hair. "Towhead that I was, I thought her dark curls were the most amazing thing I'd ever seen."

Melba hadn't heard her father ever call himself that slang word for blond-headed. Every childhood photo of him she'd ever seen showed blond hair, and she used to find his flaxen hair so very different from hers growing up. "I love that I got her hair. I used to hate it in high school. Straight hair was in and I felt like a freak."

That brought a chuckle from him. "I remember. Oh, the nights crying in the bathroom upstairs over whatever you tried this time to make it straight. I'd try to tell you that hair was the thing I loved best about your mother, but of course, that'd only make you cry harder."

"How'd you finally win her over?"

His face changed, as if the lines of his wrinkles deepened right before her eyes. He picked up a puzzle piece and was silent for a moment. "I don't remember," he said softly.

He was lying. She didn't know how she knew, but she did, and the realization stung. She wanted to call him on it, but she didn't really have that right. He was entitled to his privacy no matter how much she craved details. She tried to content herself with being glad he'd shared as much as he had, that she'd been able to see him smile over happy memories. Besides, she told herself, it was possible she was wrong and he couldn't genuinely recall.

She still craved answers. Dad just might not be the best source for information right now. It felt wrong to push her questions, to risk hurting or upsetting him again. Maybe there were other places to find the answers she sought. For now, it was time to change the subject.

"Well, I'm sure glad you did." She made her voice chipper, as if she hadn't seen the shadows pass over his face. "Hey, there's still cake left, isn't there?"

Dad smiled. "Sure is."

Melba put her knitting back into its bag and stood up. "I think there's only one thing to do about that, don't you?"

Chapter Eleven

Melba watched a heron lift gracefully from the water and fly overhead. Clutching the side of the boat as it raced around the river bend, she felt the sunshine seep into her bones. The sensation of space and freedom refreshed her, and she understood why Clark had bought the boat without a moment's hesitation. "It's like the air is bigger out here," she shouted above the engine. "Does that make any sense?"

Clark stole a glance at her as he navigated the boat toward a quiet cove. "Absolutely." His grin told her more than his shouted reply. He backed down the throttle as the boat made a sweeping arc toward shore and the engine's roar died down. "She's got the right name, don't you think?"

Escape Clause. It fit perfectly. Melba didn't want to run away from her problems, but it felt delicious to leave them behind for a brief time. Being out here in the glory of a Gordon Falls sunny spring day was exactly what her soul needed. "Perfect."

Clark ran a hand through his tousled hair, then cut the engine completely. A thick and wonderful silence settled around them. "Ah, but you haven't even gotten to the best part." He reached under the front deck, produced a small anchor, then deftly tossed it overboard and tied the rope up to the cleat with the speed of an experienced sailor. "Pull out your cell phone."

Melba couldn't think of anything she wanted to do less. "Absolutely not."

Clark grabbed her handbag and handed it to her. "No, really, pull it out."

"*Escape* and *cell phone* don't go together in my book."

Unzipping the top, Clark hovered a hand over her purse. "You don't want me to dig in here and find it myself, do you?" When Melba groaned, he added, "Please. Really, it's the best part of this whole place."

Rolling her eyes, Melba took the bag and fished out her cell. Reluctantly flipping it open, she raised an eyebrow at Clark.

"Look at the bars."

In tiny red letters, the upper corner of her screen read "X NO SERVICE." She looked up to see Clark's satisfied smile.

He spread his arms wide. "Iron-clad guaranteed silence. A tiny slice of time where no one can get to me, no one can need a thing." Tilting his head toward the sun, he pulled in a deep breath. "Escape."

Melba couldn't decide whether to inhale or gulp. A tendril of panic curled around her stomach, fighting against her lungs, which yearned to pull in a breath as deep and satisfying as Clark's. No one could reach her. The idea was as attractive as it was terrifying. "We can't stay here."

Clark settled onto the seat across from her. "No, we

can't. Not for long." He leaned in. "But think about it. For thirty minutes, no one can interrupt you. No one can hijack your day or throw another problem in your face. You have thirty minutes of absolute peace."

Peace. When was the last time she'd known anything close to peace? Even when she sat still, she was scrambling…clutching for calm, worrying, trying to stretch safety nets in every direction. Clark's words and the look in his eye pulled a craving up out of nowhere, a desperate need to soak this spot's beauty into her soul. To push the jangle of anxious noise far away? To drop the striving for even a tiny stretch of time? Oh, what a luxury that would be.

Clark seemed to see her struggle. He seemed able to read her so easily. "I'm not saying run away from your problems or all that stuff you're responsible for now. Just…drop them for a while. Long enough to catch your breath." He drew his hands up in front of his chest while he pulled in a deep breath, nodding at her.

His words made her feel starved for oxygen, as if she'd run too far too fast. Well, hadn't life made her do just that lately—run too far too fast? Melba closed her eyes and slowly, deliberately filled her lungs. The air was sweet and cool, letting light and space into all the tight places. Her exhale released knots and fears and stress. She did it once more before she opened her eyes, knowing Clark's powerful stare would meet her when she did. "The world can spare me for thirty minutes, can't it?" It seemed so obvious, almost arrogant of her to think otherwise. What was thirty minutes in the face of all that lay before her? Especially when it had done this much good in the first five minutes out here on the water?

"One more thing." Clark held up one finger while the other pulled a small drawstring bag out of a small shelf on the side of the boat. "No peeking," he said, as he set a button on his watch and then pulled it from his wrist. He dropped the watch and his cell phone into the bag. "Yours, too."

Feeling a bit foolish, Melba closed her phone and dropped it in the bag, followed by her watch. "Is that really necessary?"

"It's a ritual of sorts, I suppose." He tugged the strings shut and hung it from the speed control on the boat's dashboard. "Learned it from my chief in Detroit. For thirty minutes every morning he would go up on the roof of the firehouse. Alone. Hung his watch and pager and phone from a little bag just like this on a hook by the stair door. Everyone knew you did not go anywhere near that door when the bag was hung. He did it every day. He said it kept him sane." A flicker of shadow passed over Clark's eyes. "Kept him human in the face of…well, everything you see when you do what we do."

"Did you do it in Detroit? Go up on the roof like him?"

"Not at first. I thought it a dumb old-guy thing at first." He paused for a second, shifting his gaze out over the water before he added, "Then after, well…lots of things changed after."

She'd heard something happened to him in Detroit, some kind of accident, but had never heard exactly what occurred. Melba twisted her ring, wondering if it was okay to ask about it now.

He turned back, raising one eyebrow. "You're not going to ask 'after what?'"

"I didn't know if it was okay." A mama duck, followed by three fuzzy babies, swam into view and Melba thought about all the unasked questions waiting in the neighbors' eyes when she brought Dad, soaking wet, home from the riverbank. She knew sometimes the kindest thing to do was not to ask.

"Sometimes it isn't." Clark looked at her a long moment, shifting in his seat to face her with his arms resting on his knees. He was a bit too close—the air hummed between them in a way that had nothing to do with an outboard motor—but Melba told herself she didn't mind. "But now's okay." He broke his gaze, looking down at his hands. He fingered a scar across the back of his left hand, which made her wonder if the scar had been from his accident. He glanced up at the little blue drawstring bag.

She put her hand out. "Hey, you don't owe me any explanations."

"No," he said, touching her hand, "it's just that I'm trying to figure out if there's a version that fits into thirty minutes. This isn't the kind of story you can stop in the middle." He let his hand stay around her fingers for a moment. She felt the warmth of them, the calluses and strength, aware they'd crossed another line toward each other. Some part of her expected it to feel wrong, or at least dangerous, but it felt right. Like a little shift settling things into a new place.

She offered him an encouraging smile. "Some stories are like great black holes that way. You want to give yourself enough time to crawl out the other side."

"Yeah, like that." He seemed grateful to be understood. She knew what that was like. He gave her hand a squeeze and then released it. "Fires are like warfare—they change, grow stronger in one place and weaken in another. You're always trying to second-guess them, beat them before they beat you. When you get up into a building with more than one story, you've got to figure out where it's safe to go now and what's gonna come down around your ankles. You read the fire, like the tide." He paused before adding, "And it's always in the back of your mind what could happen if you don't get it right."

Melba sucked in a breath, her imagination casting horrid visions.

"You're trained, you've got all kinds of backup, but it's never really safe. Part of you denies that the fire is even there—you can't function if you don't forget about it on some level—but it never really goes away." Clark sat back, pulling into what she could only guess were difficult memories. "It wasn't that large a fire— fully involved, which means the whole building was going up—but not a huge structure. I could give you the whole technical rundown, but the short version is that the second floor gave out underneath me and I fell into some kind of storage container. All solid with only a top opening, kind of like a well, only square. Broke my leg in two places, and I must have hit some kind of window on the way down because I remember glass everywhere and I was bleeding."

He seemed so calm, but even his brief description set Melba's nerves on edge. She couldn't see how men and women faced that kind of thing every day. She wasn't that brave. "That's terrible."

"I wasn't on the ground two seconds before I knew, just by looking around, that there was no way out. I couldn't get myself to safety. The rest of the brigade would have to come save me." Clark shot her a smile that didn't quite mask the memory darkening his eyes. "For a guy like me, Mr. Independence, well, that just cuts right to the heart of everything, if you know what I mean. I couldn't save myself, and I'm the guy who likes to save everyone. It was my way of staying on top, of keeping in control."

"They found you and got you out." Melba said it more for herself than for him, not sure she was ready to hear grisly rescue details.

"I'm here, so yes." He stood up and walked to the back of the boat. "But believe me when I tell you it was the longest twenty-seven minutes of my life. A guy can rehash a lot in twenty-seven minutes. You can stuff a whole lot of regret into a dark box at the bottom of a fire."

It was easy to see why Clark craved wide-open spaces like the river. "That's awful to be so alone for so long."

Clark turned and sat on the edge of the boat. "Well, parts of it were. Only I don't really think I was alone. Dramatic as it sounds, I only felt alone for a little bit of it. Slowly, I came to feel…well, I don't think there's any other way to put it, but I felt God in there with me. Like He'd been waiting for me to go down far enough to wake up to the fact that He was there. To wake up and realize I couldn't ever get myself out of everything I'd fallen into." He managed a tight laugh. "Seems you have to go pretty far to make the rescue guy figure out he needs rescuing himself."

Melba looked up at him, framed in sunlight but humming with tension. It cost him something dear to revisit that time. She liked that he felt safe enough to do so with her. She liked it a lot. "I'm sorry." She couldn't think of anything else to say.

Clark came back to sit opposite her again. "Don't be. I mean, yes, it was awful, but I think I needed it. I'm not saying I had any kind of earth-shattering 'Run to Jesus' moment down there in the dark. It was more like a waking-up—which is what I did four hours later in a hospital bed—and a 'slow crawl in Jesus's direction.' I was still a lousy guy in lots of ways. But it was the tipping point for me. I started heading in the right direction after that. And, I hope, I'm still heading the right way."

"You've turned your life around, Clark. I so admire that."

He smiled, and she flushed, thinking her words right out of a bad greeting card. "Not everyone shares your view." His smile broadened and he let one finger run slowly across the back of her palm. "But thanks for the vote of confidence."

"Don't listen to those biddies. You belong here. Focus on all the good you can do."

His broad smile simmered down into something much warmer. The man's eyes were brilliant emeralds, clear with purpose...and with something else that made it hard for Melba to breathe. His fingers intertwined with hers, and Melba couldn't tell if he was pulling her toward him or if she was pulling him toward herself. He was so solid, so strong, and she felt like such a wobbly reed lately. "I don't want to be focused. Not right now. Right now I want to be distracted."

His eyes were beyond distracting. They were engulfing. A vast emerald expanse to get deliciously lost inside. "Me, too." Melba wasn't sure she actually managed to say the words out loud.

Slowly, oh so slowly, Clark slid one hand along the line of her jaw, cupping her face while his grip on her palm pulled her forward. It was as if she could taste him on the air between them even before their lips touched, and she let the sensation blot out every other thought.

When he leaned in, Melba actually kissed him first. Clark's laser-sharp intensity, the sheer vibrancy of him, filled this black hole she hadn't even realized had swallowed her. Kissing him, being kissed by him, was like gulping down life in the face of all the looming death and trauma. His touch was strong, but not fierce. Melba felt like a distinct person again—a woman with her own life, wants, and spirit—instead of just her father's guardian. When had she forgotten that life with Dad could also mean life beyond Dad's care?

Clark's slow, lingering kiss had such power in it. Not just his power, for he was the most commanding man she'd ever met, but a resurgence of her own strength. A strength that kissed him back—really kissed him back—until they both pulled away with huge breaths, looking stunned and delighted into each other's eyes.

"I've been wanting to touch your hair since I met you," he said with a smoldering grin as he wound one finger through a lock of her hair. He kissed her again, with an exquisite gentleness, then tugged on her hand until she came over to snuggle into him on the same seat. The sun, the gentle rocking of the boat, the sounds of the riverbank—it all wove together into a moment of perfection. "Wow," he sighed, and she laughed again, for she'd been having the exact same thought. *Wow.*

Melba let herself completely relax, dropped the ever-constant vigilance for a blissful bit of curling against a broad chest. There was definitely something to be said for the firefighter's physique—it felt like Clark had enough muscles to pick her up with one hand.

"Clark," she reluctantly groaned after about a couple of minutes of delicious and peaceful quiet.

"I know." He sighed. Squinting his eyes as if it caused him pain, he lifted the bag from its place over the throttle control and handed it her. "You do the honors while I drag us back to the real world." The engine rumbled to life, announcing the end of their escape.

A quick check of her cell gave her quite a shock. "Your watch didn't go off. We're running late." They'd spent nearly an hour out of cell service. Sure, Barney was with Dad, but it still made her nervous. As he hauled in the anchor, she told him, "It's nearly one."

"It'll be fine, don't worry." He turned the boat in a graceful curve back toward town. Melba found herself almost dreading the sight of Gordon Falls as it slipped into view around the bend. *Don't worry, it'll be fine,* she echoed in her thoughts.

As she handed Clark's phone back to him with a sad smile, both their phones leapt to life. Melba looked down to see four missed calls. One from the house, two from Barney's cell, and a one from the Gordon Falls Fire Department.

The snarl of words she heard from Clark told her his phone held much the same.

Chapter Twelve

They ran.

Clark docked the boat so fast he wasn't even sure he tied it up, grabbing Melba's hand as they raced up the landing to his car. She was trying to call Barney as she ran, and he was glad she didn't put up a bit of resistance when he led her to his car so he could drive. He snapped the radio on to hear it crackling with the dispatcher's voice and replies from various firefighters. Melba made a choking sound as they gave out her address.

"Dad!" She started to cry. "Oh, what's happened?"

Clark tried to think of something comforting to say, but all that came to mind was to tell her that it was probably nothing more than toast left in the toaster. He couldn't lie to her like that. Not when he recognized the codes on the radio. He grabbed the handset and identified himself as online as his tires spun the gravel out of the parking lot.

"Where are you?" came his father's furious growl. After seeing the three missed calls—all within a minute of each other—on his phone, Clark could imagine his father's angry face.

"I'm with Melba Wingate. We're on our way."

"What in the name of..." Pop never got personal over the radio...unless he was livid.

"Not now, Pop, okay?" That broke all kinds of protocol, but Clark didn't care.

He slammed at the switch on his dashboard that turned on the emergency lights and grabbed Melba's hand as he roared through town. *Dear God,* he prayed even as he heard Melba praying and punching numbers on her phone beside him. *Don't make her pay for this. Don't turn my stupidity into a giant disaster.*

As Clark pulled around the engines onto Melba's lawn, he knew enough not to be shocked by all the smoke—even the smallest fires made lots of smoke— but Melba lost her grip. "Hang on!" He tried to grab her with his eyes, do that thing he knew was his gift when rescuing, pulling victims to him, lending them his confidence. "Just hang on."

He flew around the car, reaching her as she tumbled out of the seat, not bothering to shut either door. He grabbed her hand and held it tight, scanning the site and the equipment and the sounds to get the fastest assessment of the situation as he could.

"Dad!" Melba shouted. "Where's my father?"

Jesse Sykes, his hand on a length of hose, pointed toward an ambulance to Clark's left. "There's no fire. He's okay. He's over there with Barney."

Melba pulled out of his grasp and headed toward the ambulance at a full run, and Clark let her, knowing he didn't belong in that scene right now. Jesse could tell him what he needed to know.

"Outbuilding. Old man was digging through some boxes and the place filled with smoke. Not sure how yet—maybe the wiring. Never really went up, though. The guy's rattled, got a bit of smoke inhalation, but he's mostly okay." Jesse pointed to a shed Clark could now see as they walked behind the house. Garden tools, lumber and a number of file boxes in varying states of destruction stood strewn on the grass beside it.

Clark glanced at the house's back door, the screen door still swinging open even though the inner door was shut. "Mort was out here alone?" That couldn't have been wise. Not with the way Mort had been acting lately.

"Barney said she thought he was in the living room watching television. She looked up and saw smoke coming out of the shed, and spotted the old man coming out as she was on the phone to us. He's not too sharp, I think. Kinda gone, if you know what I mean." Jesse raised one eyebrow and tapped his temple.

"I get it," Clark said, feeling sorry for Mort. He knew what it felt like to suspect people were talking about you, and he'd begun to feel a reluctant affinity for the grumpy old man, even if it was clear Mort disliked him. "Is Chad coming out?" For small and straightforward issues like this, Chad often took the role of investigator. It wasn't hard to rule out foul play here—either human error or bad wiring were most likely to blame—but an official report still needed to be filed.

"Later, I think." Jesse and Clark scanned the scene. Equipment was being loaded back onto the engines.

"Chief?" he asked tentatively, for he tried never to refer to his father in familial terms on the job. Which he wasn't. Or wasn't supposed to be. The lines between on-the-job and off-the-job weren't standing out as clean as he'd like right now.

Jesse took off his helmet and ran a hand through his dark blond hair. "Says he's not needed. I thought that's why you were here." Normally, Pop talked to the homeowners or victims involved, but evidently the chief wasn't sticking to his personal protocol in this case. It wasn't like Pop to ditch duty on account of a little personal friction, but this whole situation with Mort no longer classified as "a little personal friction."

Clark stood looking at the smoked-out shed and prayed for guidance. *What now, Lord? Do I step in or back off?* Was Pop sending him a message, or just plain ticked off? Oddly enough, it was his father's favorite childhood advice that popped into his head. *When you make a mess, clean it up.* This mess was partially his fault, wasn't it? Clark wasn't foolish enough to think he could have stopped the incident, but he'd added to Melba's distress—and his father's ire—by going AWOL in more ways than one.

"Yeah," he said to Jesse. "That's why I'm here."

Mort had looked old and frail in the hospital. Now he looked trapped and angry. As if the world had played a mean trick on him. In some way, hadn't it? When Clark approached, Mort was sitting on the edge of an ambulance, swatting away the paramedic who was trying to check him out. Barney was two steps away, shaking her head and talking to another paramedic. Melba was bouncing back and forth between them, looking more upset than he'd seen her yet. Definitely a mess.

He caught her eye for a moment, looking for permission to come closer. Sending Mort into another fit topped the list of least helpful things to do right now. Her expression didn't say much beyond sheer overload.

He'd take that over the all-out "this is your fault" he was half expecting from her. Raising an eyebrow, he waved his finger between himself and Barney. Not only could Barney give him the most useful information right now, it seemed by far the safest place to start. Melba gave a small nod and walked wearily over to her father.

"I can't remember when I've been so scared," Barney said, still shaking her head.

"Are you all right? You're not hurt?"

"Scared out of my wits, but not hurt. I been thanking the Good Lord for that every minute since, I tell you. And Mort. I don't want to think about what could have happened if I hadn't caught sight of that smoke from the kitchen window." She looked up at Clark with worried eyes.

Clark held her gaze. "You're both safe, and that's what matters. Do you think you could walk over to the back of the house with me? Tell me what you know and what you saw?" He took Barney's hand and tucked it in his elbow. "Do you have any idea why Mort was in the shed?"

"I didn't even know he'd left the house. He's not really the kind to wander off like that, and he usually asks me to go find things for him. He'd been quiet this morning, maybe a little foggy but nothing out of the ordinary." She sighed and put a hand to her chest when the shed came into view. "I couldn't tell you what was going on in that man's mind to go out there, nor whatever it was he was fixing to do inside."

"Did you ask him?"

She leveled a grandmother's glare. "What do you think? Of course I asked him what possessed him to sneak out on me and near get himself killed!"

"What did he say?"

"Oh, he thinks he answered me, but he didn't. Just gave me some angry mumbo jumbo about wanting to see if Melba had straightened up in there, which I know is no kind of answer. He didn't want to tell me. He made that clear enough."

Clark scratched his chin. "Barney, I have to ask—do you think he was trying to set it on fire?"

The glare darkened. "What kind of a question is that? Do you know how hard that man worked to keep this house after he sold off the resort? Ain't no way he wanted that to happen. He was scared, I tell you, he wasn't setting that fire, he was running from it."

"So you think this was a simple mishap?" A standard investigation would confirm that one way or another, but Clark wanted Barney's take on the incident. It seemed less painful than asking Melba the same questions.

"I'm sure of it."

"I'm sure, too." His gut told him that—and Pop always said a fireman's gut was his best equipment—but it felt good to hear that Barney hadn't seen anything to make her suspicious.

Barney turned back from the soggy shack to raise an eyebrow at Clark. "Now I got a question for you."

Clark raised an eyebrow right back.

"You treating her right? None of that old Clark foolishness going on?"

So Melba had told Barney where she was going. And who she was going with. With a pang of guilt, Clark recognized that he'd been a lot less conscientious in letting people know where he'd be, and with whom. It wouldn't matter, after he'd gotten on the radio and said he was heading to the scene along with Melba Wingate.

"Yes, ma'am," he said, not knowing what else to say. "I'm doing my best." *Doing my best to mess things up,* a snarky voice at the back of his mind added.

He was grateful for the smile that replaced Barney's glare. "Well now, that's all any of us can ask now, ain't it? I'm worried about her. She don't know half of what's coming, I think. It's gonna get rougher from here. Maybe fast, maybe not. But I never liked the idea of her facing it all by herself, far from all her city friends." A bit of the glare returned, and she wagged a thick finger at him. "Only you hear me, young man, I will not see that girl hurt. I knew her mama, and Mort gave me my first job. Jake's, too. Anyone at GFCC will tell you I will not stand for good people being hurt."

"I know." Barney's eyes could pin a man down at a hundred paces. At a full-grown twenty-eight, Clark fought the urge to gulp.

"I'm on your side," she said. "I've been defending you at church to those old hens who can't see the value in a man capable of changing his ways. Takes spine to turn your life around like that. It's gonna take spine to fill your daddy's big shoes in this town. It's gonna take spine to walk Melba through what's ahead of her."

"Barney, you've got more spine than anyone I know."

The woman had one of those warm, bubbly laughs that tumbled out of her, rich and low. "Takes one to know one, I always say." She elbowed his ribs, and Clark offered a befuddled smile. She planted her hands on her hips and blew out a breath. "Is the shed gonna have to come down?"

"I expect so. You're certainly not going to want to

let it stay cluttered up like that. I'll come by tomorrow and help Melba start sorting things out. I don't think Mort should help her—at least not at first."

"He's been complaining about the groceries I bring home. Why don't I take him out for a shopping trip and lunch at the diner? That ought to give Melba some time to sort through the worst of it."

"You're a good friend, Barney. Mort and Melba are blessed to have you."

"I'm glad to be helping out. I think maybe Melba's a bit blessed herself, if you don't mind my weighing in on the subject."

It was nice to have someone weighing in positively on whatever was going on between him and Melba. He knew what his father would say—and was probably already saying. And before that kiss on the river, he'd have argued back that they were just friends and that he had no intention of pursuing anything else. He…couldn't say that anymore. "I don't mind at all." His cell phone went off again, Pop's office number flashing on the screen. "I should probably get back."

"You going to stop and say goodbye to Melba on the way out?"

"I was thinking it might be better if I didn't. Mort got pretty upset the last time he saw me, and I don't think anyone needs more drama right now."

Barney looked back as if she could see Melba and Mort through the house. "I think you're right. I'll tell her what you said and that you'll come by tomorrow while Mort goes out with me."

"You were unreachable." Pop stood in the firehouse hallway. Even with the sounds of firefighters putting away equipment behind him, the men yelling to each other and the clang and splash of engines getting washed and restocked, Clark heard his father loud and clear as he growled the accusation.

"I was off duty and out of cell range for thir— *fifty* minutes, Pop." Clark pushed past him toward his desk. "That's not out of line." Clark knew the uselessness of that remark. Pop was never, ever off the radar where the firehouse was concerned. It used to be one of his favorite weapons when he was younger—disappearing so Pop couldn't find him—because the irresponsibility of being unreachable irritated his father so. As such, today was a deep gash in an old wound.

His father followed him, standing in the doorway with his arms crossed. "But it wasn't just you, was it?"

"Door!" It was one of his father's lines, a "Georgism" for "get in here and shut the door behind you before you say one more word." Clark had never used it on his father before, but today was evidently a day for lots of firsts. His father pulled the door shut without breaking his narrow-eyed glare. Clark glared right back. "Come on, what is this? High school, and I kept Melba out past her curfew?"

"Don't you get smart with me."

"Don't you get..." Clark chose not to finish off that thought. The painful truth was that Pop was half-right. One the one hand, Clark knew Melba was a grown woman capable of making her own decisions. On the other hand, some part of him knew he'd behaved irresponsibly. He hadn't ignored the watch on purpose, but he had a good enough sense of time to have realized they'd gone past their half-hour restriction, and he still hadn't said a word until she pulled away. His actions stood testament to how easily he slipped into even small shreds of the old Clark. He tossed his keys and his cell phone onto his desk, breaking the standoff. "I did nothing wrong today and you know it." Even as the retort left his mouth, Clark felt his own doubt cutting sharp edges into the words.

"Is that how you see it?"

"Yes, that's how I see it." Clark planted his hands on his desk chair. "And it's pretty clear that's not how you see it."

His father paused for a long moment…one of his favorite, infuriating tactics whenever they argued. "'No distractions.' Isn't that what you said?"

"This is different."

"You would always say that when I caught you not keeping your word."

Clark ran his hands through his hair. "Why are you doing this? Why are you pinning me to some ridiculous set of standards only you think necessary?"

A firefighter came up to the window in Clark's door, holding up a finger in a "Do you have a minute?" gesture. Clark shook his head and waved the man off. He looked his father straight in the eye. "Do you know what it was like to walk onto that scene today and get some insane version of 'Just wait till your dad hears about this' from men I'm supposed to lead in a few weeks' time? Do you even want me to succeed?"

Pop didn't answer. Clark couldn't tell if that was good or bad.

"I'll admit," Clark continued, grasping for some sense of reason, "that the timing was unfortunate. Awful, even. But you had no right to grouse at those guys about not being able to reach me when I was off duty and entirely within my rights not to answer my cell phone. I may have been out of line, but so were you."

"I stuck my neck out and recommended you, but you have to prove yourself..."

"No, Pop," Clark cut in. "That's just it. I *don't* have anything to prove here. I know who I am now, and how I've changed. I have the experience and the training to handle this job. These men are ready to accept me, but it won't happen until you stop throwing your weight around like this. I will do the best job I know how, but I *won't be you*." He paced back and forth behind his desk and growled, sounding entirely too much like the father in front of him. "Every time I think we've hashed this out, we're back at square one again." He looked at the chief. "I want a life outside the firehouse, Pop. I don't think that makes me a bad chief, either. Can you accept that?"

"Is that what you're saying? That being a good chief made me a bad father?"

How many times had they gone over this same raw ground? "What do you want me to say? That all the things you missed because you were here didn't matter? That I didn't hate the sound of the siren growing up? That I ran over your beeper with my motorcycle by accident? No, it wasn't perfect, but I'm here now because I've made peace with all that. I want to be chief, Pop. I do. But my kind of chief, not yours. And that means you should be more upset with the fact that Melba couldn't get to Mort than the fact that you couldn't get to me."

Pop narrowed his eyes and adjusted his baseball cap.

"He's fine, by the way. Rattled, but okay. Look, it's not like you not to ask. Whatever's gone on between you and Mort Wingate, I think maybe we need to talk about it."

His father's hands shot up. "Oh, no, we don't." The chief started toward the kitchen.

Clark followed him. "So there *is* something."

"I didn't say that." His dad had his head in the fridge again, getting ready to hide behind a root beer.

"You didn't have to. I told you Mort laid into me at the hospital. He thought Melba was her mother, which means his head was in the past. I'm starting to wonder now if he thought I was you."

His dad's only response was to pop the top off a bottle. And this time, he didn't offer one to Clark.

Heaving a sigh, Clark leaned against the counter and lowered his voice so the firemen laughing in the dining room wouldn't hear. "I like her, Pop. A lot. And I'm going to try hard not to let things get out of control because neither of us can afford it right now. But this isn't going to go away and I'd appreciate it if you'd just help me understand what's going on."

"It's water under a very old bridge and I've asked you to drop it. Let…it…go…son." It was not a request. It was a command. "If I ask you to keep clear of Melba Wingate, will you?"

Clark could think of reasons to say yes, but far more reasons to say "No."

George Bradens shook his head, fired the bottle cap into the barrel with deadly accuracy, and left the room in silence. Except, of course, for the chorus of "Hey, chief!"'s erupting as he escaped through the dining room.

Clark wanted to put his fist through the cabinet door, but let his head fall against it instead. Why did this have to be so hard?

Chapter Thirteen

Melba wrinkled her nose; the place smelled so old. The scents and sounds of this little shack felt like falling into a time warp. On the one hand, it had the atmosphere of a treasure hunt—surely among all the boxes and crates and old leather suitcases she'd find some fascinating bit of her past, some object unleashing a rush of memories. On the other hand, it was dirty and musty and not at all like she'd have expected from the tidy father who used to keep nuts and bolts sorted into labeled jars on his workbench.

Melba let out a little yelp as a too-large spider scurried away from a box of old hinges she pulled down from a sagging shelf. Practically speaking, she knew Clark was coming in a bit to help lug all this stuff out of the shack. There was something about doing parts of it alone, however. She couldn't explain her need for privacy as she picked through the boxes of old receipts and guest files. Smiling, she tucked a stack of "Wingate's Log Cabin Resort" postcards into the box she'd marked "KEEP." It had been great fun to grow up on a vacation property. Twice, a television star had come to hide away at the resort, and Melba had the delicious privilege of letting her best friends in on the juicy secret.

Tugging out a crate of garden tools, Melba's eyes hit on her mother's old sky-blue luggage. With its boxy valises and square makeup case, she could almost picture her mother getting off the train for their Niagara Falls honeymoon. Melba ran her hands over the white plastic handle—the set didn't seem at all damaged. She'd played movie star with that luggage over and over as a child, but hadn't given it a single thought in years until this moment. How many other treasures were in here waiting to be discovered?

Of course, she had to open them. How she'd loved the shiny blue lining, played for hours tucking imaginary traveling necessities into the many pockets. The first case was empty, the fabric stained from mold and time, ripping down off the lid in several places. The second case held a dank old coat with a matching hat that was probably fetching in its day, but nasty after years in confinement. Melba fished her hands in the coat pockets, bringing out a Chicago train ticket from 1983. She tucked the ticket in her own pocket before reclosing the case and dragging it and its larger partner to the lawn.

She saved the makeup case for last, hoping it held something special inside. There was a plain pink scarf—hand-knit, had Mama made it? Two hats—nothing special or worth saving, and nothing Melba could remember seeing. At the bottom, wrapped in brown paper, was a stack of something. Letters? Documents? Melba felt a small jolt of expectation raise her pulse as she pulled the twine holding the paper and spread the envelopes out on a crate.

Some had been through the mail, with canceled

stamps and military addresses. She recognized her mother's handwriting immediately, with the swirly *W*s Melba could never quite imitate. A neat, orderly version of her father's handwriting filled other envelopes— she'd forgotten how precise his handwriting had been when he was younger. Laying out the letters one by one, Melba pondered whether or not it was appropriate to open them. The urge to hoard disappearing memories warred with her parents' right to privacy. This might be her only chance to glimpse her parents as a younger couple, or even to spur some treasured stories from her father before he lost his past forever.

Halfway down the stack, a third style of handwriting startled her. Two of the letters were addressed simply to "Maria," obviously hand-delivered rather than posted through the mail. One other was addressed to her at the resort from an address in Chicago, typewritten with "CONFIDENTIAL" in capital letters on the lower corner. All the letters were from fall of 1984, from her father's final tour of service somewhere in the Persian Gulf. Medical information? Some legal matter? She felt better about looking in this envelope rather than her parents' private correspondence.

The letter inside wasn't official. It was handwritten, two pages filled on both sides, and signed simply "G." Who was "G"?

"Melba?" Clark's voice yanked her from her thoughts. "You in there?"

She'd half considered calling Clark and telling him not to stop by. Part of her was angry, wanting to blame him for her being out of cell range when things had escalated. But she knew that was a cheap out. She'd agreed—readily, in fact—to the escape down the river with him. She was perfectly capable of insisting she keep her watch and return after the prescribed thirty minutes. She'd chosen their actions just as much as Clark had. If she was honest, a larger part of her couldn't wait to see him again, to soak in the extraordinary strength that seemed to seep into her when she was with him. "Here," she called, laying down the letter and walking out into the sunshine.

"How's the cleanup going?" Clark reached for her hand and she let him take it. She'd forgotten the simple wonder of having someone hold your hand. "Doesn't look so bad so far."

"Actually—" she felt herself smile, the sensation foreign but welcome "—it's been a bit of an adventure. Lots of junk but some neat stuff I'll want to save." She nodded toward the box and they both crouched over it. "Look at these." She held up the postcards.

Clark chuckled at the cheesy photos and bold "Wish You Were Here" lettering splashed across the front. "Wow. You definitely need to do something with these." He peered at the cards. "I'd almost forgotten what the place looked like." He squinted at one card. "Hey, is that you?"

Melba took the card to spy the little girl with a fat pink ribbon in her hair standing next to one of the too-clean sheep. The sheep that grazed over her parents' resort looked snowy white and cuddly in the photo, but hardly ever like that in real life. Mama had fussed for hours to get that sheep looking like something out of a children's book, and it had been dirty and tangled with burrs again the next day. The memory of taking that photo, of feeling like a princess getting her picture on a postcard, raised a lump in her throat. "I think I was five. I'd forgotten we even had these made." Melba stepped back into the shed, seeing it like the treasure trove she'd hoped it would be. "I'm so glad we didn't lose the shed. It's messy, but there's still so much stuff in here."

Clark peered around. "My dad always said burning buildings were sad, but lost possessions were worse." He pointed to the stack of envelopes. "Letters?"

"From when my parents wrote to each other during the war. They were in my mom's makeup case, tied up all neat like a present."

"Have you looked at them?" Clark ran his hands over one of the suitcase's clunky brass latches.

"Not yet. Feels a bit like prying, you know?"

"I suppose it would."

"There's one, though, I can't quite figure out. I haven't read anything but the signature yet, but I don't have any relatives with names that start with *G*."

Clark leaned in, studying the envelope while Melba still held the letters. "Wait a minute." He shook his head. "No, it's nothing."

"What?"

"Nothing." Clark motioned toward the letter. "What does Mr. G say?"

Melba raised an eyebrow. "How do you know it's *Mr.* G?"

"I don't. Just looks like a man's handwriting, I suppose. Grandpa, maybe?"

"No, Mom called her grandfather Poppy. She talked about him a lot. Since her own father—my grandfather—died when he was young, Poppy was in her life a lot." Melba sat down on a crate. "It's dated November

1984. 'My dearest Maria.'" Melba looked up at Clark. "'Dearest'?"

Clark stared back with a puzzled look on his face and found an overturned bucket to sit down upon.

Melba read on.

"I know you're worried, but I'm so glad you came to me for help. Don't ever call yourself bad for what's happened. War is a terrible thing and it causes terrible things to happen, even off the battlefield. No matter what Mort says or does, know that I will always be there for you. Always."

Melba stared at the letter, feeling the room spin a bit as it sunk in what she might actually be reading. She gulped down a breath as her eyes scanned back up to the date. 1984. The fall before her birthday. "Oh, Lord." It was the start of a panicked prayer, but she didn't even know what she was praying for.

"Maybe I shouldn't be here," Clark said softly.

"No." Melba held out a hand. "No, please don't go."

"Are you sure?"

"Yeah," she said, not sure of anything. "Don't go."

Melba returned to the letter, only to realize her hands were shaking.

"You need to take care of yourself now. You and the baby. I have taken care of everything else."

She looked up at Clark. "The baby. Clark, that's *me*. This letter is dated eight months before my birthday."

Melba continued to read.

"Danny Baker won't cause you any trouble. He will never return to Gordon Falls, never claim the child. He's not much of a man to be so easily persuaded to leave, I'm sorry to say. I'll never understand, my dear Maria, why you would give yourself to such a scoundrel when I've waited so long for you. You broke my heart, and still I can't turn from you when you're in such need. It's the worst pain to know he's had even one night with you when I have had nothing."

She reached the bottom of the page, dreading what other earth-shattering news might lie on the other side. Melba shut her eyes, tried to force air into her collapsing lungs. So it was true. Mort Wingate wasn't her father. Her father was some faceless man named Danny Baker. Her past was a knot of lies and secrets tying her to a complete stranger.

Her hands shook as she turned the page.

"If Mort is the man you claim he is, then he will not turn you out. And while this is the only time I will ever speak of this, I hope he does."

Melba's hand went to her throat at the words, which were underlined.

"For you already know that I would leave her— yes, I would leave my wife—to make a life with you without a second's hesitation. Even after all these years, I can't stop loving you. I know you know that or you would have never come to me with all this. You know I'd do anything to make you happy. If that means staying with Mort, then so be it.

"My only condition is that he must know. I've arranged so that no one else will ever suspect, but Mort will be told—by me if not by you. If he's honorable enough to stick with your marriage, I won't step in. It'll kill me, but I'll stand by. What I won't stand by and watch, however, is him having what I would hold so dear on account of a lie.

"You have my word, I'll never say anything to anyone if you stay with Mort. Just one word from you, though, and we'll go anywhere you want and make a fresh start. You can bank on that, you and the baby.

"I've always loved you. More than him, even if you can't see it.—G."

Clark felt wildly ill at ease, as if he'd stumbled into some private place he didn't belong. This was worse than witnessing Melba's struggles with Mort. It was like watching someone's soul splayed out in raw pain. Firefighting made him used to seeing people at their worst. He was accustomed to people at the end of their wits in terrible crises, but this was so different. He had no training to cope with this kind of shock, this emotional burn. He felt helpless to guide Melba down the face of the huge, steep gorge that had now opened up in her life. Why had God thrust him to the edge of it alongside her with no warning? Clark didn't know what to do with that. "I'm sorry." The words tumbled out of him, inadequate and useless. "I'm really sorry."

"It's real." Her fingers buried themselves in her hair, as if she could hold the storm of worry in with her hands. "It's right here. I think I was pretending it wasn't, that it was just Dad losing it, but…" She swiped a tear away with the back of her hand. "It's true. He's not my father."

Clark didn't want to leave her like this, but he also knew he had to get out of there. He had to find some way to make an escape before Melba asked…

"And who on earth is this G?"

Aw, come on, Lord, was that really necessary? Clark felt as trapped at the bottom of a dark hole as clearly as he had that night at the fire.

"I mean, where did he come from? Mom and Dad were married and he's in there messing with everything and telling her things like 'I've always loved you.'" Melba's voice began to pitch higher with anger. Who wouldn't be angry? The woman's life had been turned inside out within the space of a month.

He didn't have to, but he asked anyway, "Can I see the letter?" As she handed him the envelope, he instinctively handed her a tissue from his pocket.… Chief Bradens insisted every firefighter carry tissues or handkerchiefs in their uniform as a gesture of decency because they so often came upon people in tears. He'd never been able to leave the house without tucking one in his pants pocket. Melba had used four of his since they'd met.

Clark stood up, pretending to need more light to see the letter. The shack was feeling close and tight, the air suddenly holding too much dust. He heard Melba sniffle behind him, and he turned for a second—truly, his glance had a "last look" feel to it—and watched her dab her eyes. They'd be linked—or maybe they'd be separated—by what he said next. Actually, Clark realized they were already linked in some way, and they'd go on being linked whether he spoke what he saw or not. But inevitably this would place a barrier between them as well.

The scan of the letter wasn't really necessary. More of a stalling tactic, if Clark was honest with himself. He'd recognized already, had gotten a short glimpse of the single-letter signature. There wasn't any use in trying to deny it: no one made *G*s the way his father did. It was a younger, stronger version, but inarguably his father's. Pop was "G."

Chapter Fourteen

For a moment, Clark tried to tell himself he wasn't really sure. He could couch it like a hunch, give both of them a measure of false hope, stall the dangerous news the way he'd been taught to do with victims in crisis. Still, could he even pretend to deny why God had orchestrated his presence here at this particular moment? Did he have any right to withhold the truth when she seemed so besieged by missing information? He stared for a second, unable to decide if it was more cruel to tell her or to withhold the facts.

"Why do there have to be so many secrets?" Melba sighed behind him. "What's the point?"

"I don't know, Melba." It was a half-truth. He really didn't understand the point of the mountain of lies piling up in front of him. Clark refolded the letter, the "I will always love you" cruelly showing up as the last thing he saw before tucking it back in the envelope. He sat down and took Melba's hand, laying the letter in her upturned palm. "But, I suppose you know for sure now, instead of all that guessing. I suppose that's something."

Her face pinched in anger. He couldn't blame her.

Parts of him were boiling up even as they spoke, and he was going to need to get out of there soon. "Something? It's something, all right. All these years, and four people knew the truth about me, but not one of them ever let me know." She looked up at him, her eyes wild and wide. "And maybe it's more than just four. Maybe loads of people know, and they've been whispering behind my back all these years."

"I can't think that's true." It couldn't be. Pop wouldn't stand for it. He'd promised Melba's mother that he wouldn't let word spread. Of course, he'd also promised Clark's own mother to love, honor and protect her for as long as they lived, and yet here he was, just a few years after his own marriage, offering to run away with another woman. Clark bit down on the argument erupting inside of him. "Your parents loved you."

"You don't lie to people you love. *I* don't lie to people I love."

She chose the worst possible words, for while Clark realized he was falling for Melba, he wouldn't tell her what he suspected. Not now. And who was he kidding? He "suspected" nothing. He knew. She'd probably never forgive his silence right now, but he couldn't speak up. He just couldn't make the words come out from under all that anger.

She shot up off the bench, shaking her head. "Whoa there." He lunged after her, catching her elbow. "Hang on a minute."

She pulled from his grasp, wheeling on him. "Hang on a minute? For what?"

"You've had a shock. You need time to think this through."

"Dad knew!" She spat the words out. "They both

knew. All those years, even when I was old enough to handle stuff like this. This was the eighties, for crying out loud, not the Victorian age."

"Melba." Clark grabbed her hand and tried to hold her wildly shifting gaze with his eyes. "We don't know anything for sure."

"We?" she snarled.

That slip told him he was in trouble here. "Okay, poor choice of words. This is happening to you, I get that." Despite his words, he couldn't let on how his own world had just tilted. It was no fun to learn your father held a lifelong torch for someone who wasn't your mother. He let go of Melba's arm to run a hand down his own face. "Just don't haul off without thinking." Thinking? Thoughts were exploding in Clark's brain like shrapnel. Pop had been married to Mom when he wrote that. Pop had been ready to leave Mom—and *him,* Clark realized with a start, remembering the date on the letter—for Maria when he wrote that. None of that matched up with the man Clark called father, and suddenly everything looked like lies. "I think you need to take a minute before…"

"Before what? I make it worse?" She flung her arms wide, curls falling into her angry face. "Explain to me, Clark, just *how* this could get worse?"

Clark knew exactly how this could get worse. *Lord, please, show me I'm wrong.* He wasn't. The column of ice running down his back told him he wasn't, that he'd have to tell her what he knew and live with the consequences. Only not now. Not when he was still reeling himself.

"I'm showing this to Dad. I'm done with all the lies."

"Melba, don't do that. Give yourself a minute to

think. To pray, even." Oh, that was a low blow, Clark chided himself. *How dare you bring God into this as if you're the righteous one when you're standing here withholding what you know.*

"I don't need a minute." She headed back toward the house.

Tell her. It will only get worse, his conscience hollered at him. "Melba, stop." He lunged after her again, and the pain in her eyes when she turned cut his heart to ribbons. The urge to tell her the truth was almost choking him, but he couldn't manage to form the words. Instead, he tried to stall. "C'mon, Melba, just hang on a minute. Think about your Dad. You can't just slam into him with this—he's not up to it or he'd have told you earlier."

"Not up to it? I don't care whether or not he's up to it. I haven't been up to any of this and no one's asked me if I was ready!"

"I know." He couldn't add to her pain right now. Cowardly or not, he couldn't hand her a reason to turn from him. Instead, he pulled her to him, and she crumpled into his arms. It should have been wonderful to have her cling to him like that, but it felt terrible.

"I was lied to." She cried into his shoulder. "By the people who are supposed to love me most. You know what it sounds like to me? Like this 'G' person sent my biological father away. Swept him under the rug like a…a…like I was some kind of ugly mistake that would mess up everybody's plans. Do you have any idea what that feels like?"

Clark felt the anger and betrayal unwinding his composure. The guy who messed up everybody's plans, who did what he wanted and never stopped to consider the consequences? Oh, Clark had loads of experience with what that felt like. He'd heard it nearly every day of high school: *"Chief Bradens's son should never act like this."* Act like what? Like the disloyal schemer who wrote that letter? All those respectability proclamations rang so false right now that his gut was roiling from the dissonance. "Your dad's not even home right now, remember? It's going to take some thought on how to talk to Mort about this."

"'Mort.'" She pulled out of his embrace, her hands twisting through her hair again. "Do I call him Dad? It's like I don't know what to do about anything or what's even real."

"He's still your father."

"Easy for you to say." She was mad at the whole world right now, and he couldn't blame her.

Still, this couldn't have come as a complete shock—she'd already suspected as much before seeing the letter. Clark fisted his hands in frustration, trying to remind himself she didn't know what he knew. "I think," he said as calmly as he could manage, "you shouldn't talk to your father…"

"Which one?" she cut in.

"Mort. I think you shouldn't talk to Mort just yet." It was getting harder to stay calm, and he had selfish reasons to not let her confront her father until he knew more. "Has it occurred to you that Mort might not know about what went on between this 'G' person and your mom? Do you really want to hand that to him now? Do you want your last months with him to be about this?" The more Clark thought about this, the worse Pop was starting to look. The roiling in his stomach was solidifying into a tight ball of disgust. All the speeches about conduct and honor. All the lectures about family name. What a pack of lies.

Melba put one foot on her front steps. He could see white knuckles on her hands as they clung to the railing. It was the same stance of weary pain he'd seen when he'd found her with her head against the vending machine. He knew she was trying to do the right thing but it must have felt to her like God was just heaping pain upon pain. Where was the mercy in that?

"I'd like to be alone."

She looked like a woman ready to do something drastic. Something hugely regrettable. "Promise me you won't go to your father until I talk you through this again."

"Why should I promise you anything?"

Clark threw his hands up in the air, annoyed because she was right. "Because I'm trying to help." Help? How did keeping the truth from her help?

She turned to him then, her eyes dark and angry. "Thanks for your help, Clark, but I think you should leave."

"Melba…"

The door shut in his face. A man of honor would have pushed open the door and told her what he knew, explained why he needed her to wait.

Yes, well, we've all learned just what kind of men of honor Bradens men are, haven't we? Clark swallowed the urge to punch something, someone, and stomped back to his car.

Clark slumped on the front steps of Pop's house an hour later, sweaty and out of breath. In a desperate scramble for control, he'd gone on a five-mile run—

the first mile at a full-tilt angry sprint, no less—to clear
his head before he saw his father. It hadn't worked. He
was still angry—fuming, actually—but the physical
boiling in his gut had died down enough to allow the
slim hope of a productive conversation.

Hold me back, Lord, Clark prayed. He'd tried to lay
the whole situation out before God as he ran. That was
the way he wrestled with things now, to pray it out piece
by piece as he ran, but it failed him this time. Clark
never got any further than "hold me back," fully aware
of the way that the wave of built-up anger, the years of
judgment, the glares of disappointment all pressed hard
against his control. *I have to try to get this untangled.
There's no hope of my doing that without Your grace
right now.* Taking one more deep breath and wiping his
forehead with the hem of his T-shirt, Clark knocked on
Pop's door.

The frown on his father's face when he pulled open
the door to see Clark—red in the face and dripping
sweat—didn't help matters. "Your shower broken?" It
was only half a joke.

"I need to talk to you. Alone." It was near dinner-
time, and Pop often had buddies over for dinner. The
smell of barbecue chicken wafted out of the doorway.

"Nobody here but us chickens," Pop chuckled.

Clark didn't laugh as he walked in behind his dad. He
headed straight for the kitchen, wanting to put a counter
or a table between him and Pop for this conversation.

"Sounds serious." Pop lifted the lid on a saucepan,
stirred something, then replaced the lid. "Sit down."

"I'd rather stand."

That got the chief's attention. Pop lowered one eyebrow and eyed Clark carefully as he eased himself into

his favorite chair at the end of the table. Clark's mind flashed reluctantly back to family dinners around the table, only now while the details were all postcard-perfect, everything felt hollow, shellacked to be shiny where it wasn't.

No sense beating around the bush. "What happened between you and Maria Wingate?"

Pop narrowed his eyes. "What kind of a question is that?"

"Melba found a letter as she was cleaning out the shack at Mort's place today. It's got your signature on it, and it's pretty clear there was something—a lot of somethings—going on." Clark held his father's eyes. "Can you please not snowball me on this? Will you give me that much?" He wanted to yell, to stand over his father and threaten all kinds of things, but had promised himself the decency of asking for Pop's voluntary co-operation.

Pop sat still for a long moment, then let out a sigh and pinched the bridge of his nose. He cursed under his breath, something Clark had never heard his father do. "I suppose," Pop said in a tight, quiet voice, "I was an idiot for thinking it would never surface one day. To Melba, that is." His gaze flicked up to Clark. "But you? I didn't see that coming."

Clark felt the choking press of "it's real" he'd seen come over Melba, a knot of sour confirmation cutting off his breath. "I know I didn't," he said, not caring how sharp he cut the edges of his words.

"I never figured Maria would keep that letter. She should have burned it. She was never smart about those kinds of things, impulsive and emotional." Despite the censure in his words his tone was warm, fond.

It made Clark nuts to hear his father talking about someone else's wife like that. He paced the room, trying to keep a lid on his anger. "I saw the date. You were married to Mom when you wrote that. You were my father when you wrote that! How could you even live with yourself, lying to Mom?"

"She knew."

Clark planted his hands on the table, leaning in to glare into his father's eyes. "What?"

"Well, not about Danny Baker—no one was ever supposed to know about that. But she knew how I felt about Maria when she asked me to marry her."

Clark's knees gave way beneath him and he sunk into a chair. Mom always told of Pop's proposal down on one knee on the bridge by the river at sunset—the kind of gooey, fairy-tale details that used to make him groan in middle school. "But…"

Pop waved his hand as if the facts were inconsequential. "I told her she could make up whatever story she liked. Folks would never sit well with her asking me back then. Her father's drinking was out of control and she was desperate to get out of the house—and she loved me. I did love her…in time. And she loved you so much. You were born two days after her father died. 'My new life,' she called you. Always said you were what saved her. It was never really me."

Clark felt like he'd been hurled off a cliff, still tumbling in the air. "So it would've been just fine for you to walk away if Maria Wingate would have you?" His father's calm—so calm it was bordering on relief—was infuriating. "How is this okay? How is *any* of this okay?" He jabbed a finger at Pop. "How could you stand

there and lecture me on honor and family name knowing you'd done this?"

"I know what you must think of me…"

"Oh, no, you don't." Clark shot up off the table to
pace the kitchen. "You don't want to know what I think
of you right now."

"I was never unfaithful to your mother after that."
Pop's voice rose but Clark wouldn't even give him the
satisfaction of turning around. "Mort agreed to raise the
baby as his own and Maria chose to stay with Mort, so
that was the end of it. Your mother and I found a way
to build a life—not a perfect life but good enough. You
were loved, even when you made a mess of things."

It all made a sick sort of sense now. The obsessive
dedication to the firehouse. Why his mother put up with
it all those years. The frost between Pop and any of the
Wingates. Clark felt like someone had taken a knife to
all his childhood memories and slashed a gaping hole
in the canvas. "Yes, I was such a disappointment to a
fine upstanding man like you. How could you lecture
me about Lyla?"

"Because Lyla was married!"

Lyla had been one of the low points of Clark's rebellious youth. He'd been flat-out in love with her when
she'd admitted to him she was married, that she was
leaving her husband. That whole month was a storm of
sin and pain and flying in the face of everything Clark
knew was right. "Yeah, well, we all see where I get it
from, don't we?"

His father's face burned red with anger. "I was never
with Maria when she was married to Mort. For years,
we never went near each other, never even shook hands.
Not even when Mort went off to the Middle East. Then

she came to me, Clark, desperate for help, sure Mort would throw her out for the mistake she'd made."

"And that's exactly what you wanted, isn't it? You ran off her lover so he'd be out of the picture, and then you insisted she tell Mort, hoping you'd be right there to rescue her when he tossed her aside." It stung so badly, reminding him of the nights Clark had offered to run away with Lyla. What a mess he'd made of his life before God had finally shaken him to his senses.

"I admit some part of me hoped that would happen. Paying off Danny Baker wasn't the smartest thing I ever did, but I didn't have a lot of options."

Clark felt his world tumble a little farther down the cliff. "You what? You *paid* Melba's biological father to disappear?" He glared at his father, not even recognizing the man sitting at the table. The whole thing sounded so underhanded, so opposite of every value his father claimed to hold. "What else don't I know? Come clean now, Pop, 'cause I'm not sure I can handle another round of this."

"He was a cad, a low-life fireman I never liked. Took advantage of Maria one night when she got word Mort had been wounded in the Gulf. She was like that, Maria was. Strong one minute, falling apart at the next. She came to me in hysterics when she realized she was pregnant and that Danny was most likely the father."

Anger was boiling up in Clark's gut, making him want to take a swing at the whole world. "She came to you." He said it like an accusation, not a fact.

Pop shot him a dangerous look. "Take a minute, if you can, to think about what that felt like. To have a woman you've loved your entire life come and ask you to help her get out of a jam like that. To know she let herself be taken in by a jerk like that but yet she'd refused you. And even after everything that had happened, the thing that truly scared her was losing the love of the man she'd chosen over you in the first place. Give me a little credit for helping her when she punched me in the gut."

Clark was not interested in giving Pop one ounce of credit. "You were *married to Mom* at the time! I'm supposed to think this was noble?"

"I'm not proud of it, but you of all people know life isn't neat and perfect. How many times have I bailed you out of a hole you'd dug yourself into?"

"This isn't about me. Don't make this about me." The wind knocked out of him when Clark remembered to ask, "You said Mom knew. Knew what? How you felt about Maria? What you'd done? What you *offered* to do?"

"Never the details. She knew something had happened, but to her credit she never asked. I don't think she wanted to know."

"Imagine not wanting to know your husband paid off some lowlife to disappear and was ready to run off with another man's pregnant wife." Clark made sure every word cut sharp and harsh. "It boggles the mind."

"That's enough!" Pop fired back, pushing himself up out of the chair to walk away and kill the heat under the saucepan with an angry snap of the stove dial. "I'm sorry you found out. I'm sorry I no longer measure up for you. Grow up and see this for what it is…a terrible mistake made by wounded folks in a tight spot." He turned to look at Clark, suddenly looking like an old, hollow man. "The world is full of things we all regret and can't fix, Clark. It's the whole point of grace."

Chapter Fifteen

Dinner had been a mess. Melba had been an angry ball of confusion all afternoon, snapping at Dad for no reason at all and every reason under the sun. Dad didn't know why she was upset, but he was responding to the tension all the same. He had insisted he didn't like chicken cacciatore when Melba—and even Barney— knew it was his favorite dish. Despite the bickering over dinner and everything else, she couldn't bring herself to talk to Dad about the letter, despite her threats to Clark. It was all still too tangled in her brain.

How much did he know? Had Mom told him just because G had demanded it for his help, or because she thought the truth was important between a husband and a wife? Worse yet, did Dad know the full story of G's involvement, or just that his wife had made a terrible mistake?

Melba caught herself on those words as she snapped off the kitchen light and headed for the stairs. "Terrible mistake?" *She* was that terrible mistake—or at least the consequence of it. It made her feel worthless, even though she knew better. *Oh, Lord,* she prayed as she hauled herself up the steps, finding them twice as steep as usual tonight, *I'm lost here. I don't know what to do or feel or think.*

Pinocchio followed her up the stairs, jumping up to join her on the bed as she lay back and stared blankly at the yellow canopy. He swatted at a tassel dangling from the bookmark in her Bible, and she reached for the book. "You always were a smart cat." She ran her hand down his back, managing a smile when he arched into her palm and purred. "Calling Charlotte would take an hour of explanation and this is definitely a God-sized problem."

The bookmark was where it always was, in Psalm 139. The artist in Melba loved the poetry of the psalms, the passion and full depth of David's emotions spilled out on the page. She began to pray her way through it, the way she always did. *"You hem me in behind and before, and You lay Your hand upon me." I need to feel You all around me tonight, Lord. I feel like I'm nowhere, like I'm nobody. It feels impossible to know Your hand's upon me right now. Hem me in so I don't do something I can't take back.*

She wanted to take back the way she'd treated Clark. He'd walked in on her emotional land mine—walked in on several of them, for that matter—and that wasn't his fault. *I'm sorry for that,* she confessed to God, *and I have no idea how to fix it. Are You trying to show me that I'm too fragile to have a relationship right now?*

She read on: *"even the darkness will not be dark to You, the night will shine like the day, for darkness is as light to You."* No matter how dark all these secrets seemed, they weren't darkness to God. They weren't even a surprise. He'd known her entire life who she was and how she'd come into the world. It was no coincidence that the next verses were her favorites: *"For You created my inmost being; You knit me together in my mother's womb. I praise You because I am fearfully and wonderfully made."* She was no fluke of circumstance, no horrid misstep's outcome. God knew exactly who she was. Every detail. Sure, things didn't line up into ideal circumstances, and it would still take a long while for all this secrecy to settle in her soul, but God loved her not one bit less today than He had yesterday. "The same is true of Dad, isn't it?" she asked aloud, more to God than to Pinocchio. Wasn't that more reason to admire her father, to love him for loving her even when biology and morality handed him reasons to dismiss her?

Melba thought of a scarf she'd knit recently, a complicated pattern called entrelac. The first rows of the pattern made all these squares and triangles that appeared as if they couldn't possibly fit into one whole. And if she'd stopped where her doubts were strongest— in the pattern's early stages—they never would have meshed. She had to find the next instruction and follow it. *What is that step, Lord? I don't have a life pattern. I don't know where to look next.*

She stayed in the best place she knew—wandering through one Psalm after another—until the text-message alert on her cell phone chirped an incoming message.

Meet me. The message was from Clark.

Melba rolled over and stared at the cat. "That's what I get for praying for a next step. One I don't want to take."

I can't leave, she typed in reply. It wasn't a no, but it wasn't a yes, either.

You don't have to. I'm in your driveway.

Feeling way too much like a teenager, Melba walked to the window and pushed aside the drapes to make out the lines of Clark's dark blue sports car and a flash of his red hair inside.

"I wasn't sure you'd come out," Clark said when she pulled open the door and ventured out onto the steps. He looked terrible. The energy was gone from his face, and his shoulders slumped under a ratty GFVFD sweatshirt.

"I wasn't sure I would, either." She zipped up the neck on her fleece pullover. The night was crisp, but not uncomfortable. That was good, because she wasn't about to let him inside. "You look awful."

"It hasn't been the best of days." He looked at her, and for the first time she saw the control stripped from his eyes. As if the afternoon had peeled off all the "hero" to leave an open wound underneath.

"Did something happen at the firehouse?"

"Can we just not talk about it?" He sat down on the step at her feet, leaning his back against the railing. "I can't stand how we left it this afternoon." He ran his hand through his hair. "I don't know what to do or what to say. I don't know how to help or even if I should. All I know is that I want to help untangle all of this for you." He looked up at her. "And I know that makes no sense but none of this makes sense anyways."

"No, it doesn't." Melba sat down on the step opposite him. "It's like Dad and all of this have stomped on every sore spot I own. I hate secrets. You can't possibly know how much I hate secrets."

His eyes narrowed. "Why so much?"

Melba pulled in a deep breath. "You know my mom died of cancer two years ago. She'd been sick for a couple of years before that. It was an aggressive cancer. She actually got more time than anyone expected—although I didn't find that out until later. I made all this noise after design school about wanting to travel the world. It's actually why I got into the textile business—lots of importing to do. I made lots of plans, always dreaming about something on a round-the-world scale. Turns out, Mom and Dad kept her cancer from me for as long as they could, thinking they'd keep me from traveling if they told me."

"Did you? Travel, I mean?"

"That's just it…I didn't go, but not because of some kind of imagined parental guilt trip." She felt her chest tighten, just thinking about the night she learned her mom was terminal. "You know how you are just starting out, so sure you've got all the time in the world. I just fiddled away that time, not doing anything, really." She squinted her eyes shut. "I would have spent those years so differently if I'd known they were mom's last." She opened her eyes again, grateful to see a gush of emotion in Clark's eyes. He understood regret, he got the cost of wasted years. "I know we couldn't have gone around the world, but we could have had some adventures together. By the time they couldn't hide it from me anymore, she was too sick to do anything."

He didn't say anything at first, but she could tell he empathized with her pain. When was the last time she'd met a man who was such a good listener? What a gift he was. "How did you find out?" he asked after a long moment.

"I was home for a long weekend visit and I ran out of aspirin. Rather than bother them downstairs, I just went into their bathroom and started rooting through the drawers." She fiddled with the zipper pull on her jacket, the vivid image sending ice down her spine as if it had been last week instead of years ago. "When you see a dozen prescription bottles and some of them say 'post-radiation,' it doesn't take a master's degree to figure out why your mom's been losing so much weight lately."

"That had to be rough."

"We had such a fight that night," Melba said, peeking in at the warm glow of the living room curtains. "It's the only time I've ever seen my dad cry…before the funeral, that is." She felt the anger rise again. "I made them both promise me that night not to keep anything from me ever again. How could they do that? How could they stand there—both of them—and promise me that, knowing there was still such a big secret between us?" She looked at Clark. "You don't do that to people you love. You just don't."

He was so bad for her. He was everything she hated in relationships all wrapped up into one smitten guy. Sure, that sounded like something out of a romantic comedy, but his life was feeling like some kind of surreal movie anyway. He couldn't stay away. He couldn't tell her, but he couldn't not be near her. It was wrong, hurtful even, but he seemed powerless after the way Pop had tangled his thoughts and his past. The need to be near Melba—to find some sense of balance in her brown eyes and know she wasn't tumbling off the edge of some cliff like he felt he was—hummed through him when he'd gone home after arguing with Pop. He'd showered, stumbled around the house for half an hour, and then, even though he knew a dozen reasons why he shouldn't, Clark had simply given in and driven here.

"All that, piled on top of all this. That's too much

pain. I'm worried about you." *I'm worried about me, too.* Clark knew of men who feared becoming like their fathers. That made sense. Coming undone because you've discovered your father is *just like you?* Or at least, just like the messed-up man you used to be? Maybe still are? That made no sense at all.

"I'm angry one minute, just sort of hollowed out the next." Melba's voice caught as she leaned against the opposite railing on her dad's house steps. They had so much in common. Only she didn't know that yet. It was a cruel paradox—he felt so close to her but could hurt her so deeply.

Tell her. No, don't. You need to. She needs more time. He watched her twist one of her rings and yearned to thread his fingers through hers and hold her hand. The war in his conscience was shredding him to pieces, and all Clark wanted to do was hold her and kiss her until the feel of her silenced the shouting in his head.

He managed to squelch the impulse to touch her for all of one minute, then reached over and offered his open hand to her. Clark physically felt his heart drop when she did not respond. Then, just as he was about to withdraw it, she laid her hand in his open palm. "I'm sorry I yelled for you to leave." She said it quietly. "This isn't your fault."

Ouch. Clark pushed out a sigh. "I can't figure out whose fault it is, or if it even matters." That wasn't completely true. He knew whose fault at least some of it was and—to him, at least—it mattered a whole lot. Pop would have rewritten all their histories in a heartbeat if Maria had said yes to his offer to run away together, and that felt despicable to him. He started to think, *What kind of man tempts a woman out of her marriage?* only to realize he'd done the same thing to Lyla. That made him just as despicable. And really, what was more despicable than what he was doing now, not telling Melba what he knew?

Melba lifted her face to the starlit night. The burgundy color of her jacket did something glowing to her skin under the moonlight; gave her a creamy, spicy quality that made his head spin. He followed her gaze up to the broad wash of stars filling the night sky. Detroit's smoggy sky never let him see the stars, even when he went up on the station roof. Here, they were always dazzling. She wrapped her free hand around tucked-up knees. "I keep asking God where He is in all this."

Her voice wavered some more, and Clark felt the desire to pull her close surge up stronger than ever. Instead, he offered her hand a slight squeeze and asked, "And?"

She returned her eyes to him. "And the answer I get is 'right here,' only I can't much feel it. Not where I need to."

"*I'm* right here," he blurted out as that "rescue me" look undid his heart and ran off with every sensible thought. Hearing himself, Clark banged his head on the railing behind him. "Wow, that was incredibly stupid, wasn't it? I'm not God. For crying out loud, Melba, I'm the *last* thing you need."

Melba shifted across the steps to settle in beside him, and he felt something enormous slide from his shoulders when she laid her head there. "But you are right here. Maybe—" she curled in under his shoulder and Clark lost his heart right there "—maybe you're just what I need."

He'd take the scent of her hair to his grave. He'd

fallen so hard so fast, this could never be anything but disaster. *Oh, God, don't let me hurt her,* Clark prayed, knowing he'd do just about anything to keep her, even stupid and wrong things. Were it not for her, he probably would have driven away from Pop's right onto the highway and kept going. Clark couldn't stop himself from leaving several soft kisses in her curls. *I can't tell her. Not yet,* he pleaded with God, desperately aware of his weakness. *You have to fix this—I don't know how.*

Melba turned her face toward him, sliding her arms around his neck and stealing any control he had left. She kissed him with an abandon some part of him knew wasn't her true nature. She was reacting, reeling from what the day had thrown at her. The firefighter in him knew this, recognized it for what it was, but the man in him gladly drowned in it. Welcomed it, reveled in it. She was exquisite, filling some part of him he hadn't even realized had gone empty. It'd be so easy to lose himself in her right now. After all, why bother doing the right thing when no one else seemed to put forth the effort?

The right thing? Had he lost his ability to even know what that was?

"Hey," he gasped, pulling her hand from his neck. "What I think you need is for me to go." The lure of her clinging to him was about to pull him under.

"Yeah," she said, pulling back, a little of the old Melba coming back to her features. "Yeah."

It hurt—it physically hurt—to slide himself from her arms. "But hold that thought," he said, allowing himself a wry smirk. "That was a mighty fine kiss. And I don't know what that is you put in your hair, but the smell of that stuff reduces a man to a puddle of bad ideas." His father's words came back to him, hitting him like a bucket of ice. *She was never smart about those kinds of things, impulsive and emotional.* He'd come a whole lot closer to disaster than he'd realized. "Believe me, I should go right *now.*"

She stood up, the chill of the night air swirling around them. "You're right. I'm…"

"Don't say 'sorry,'" he interrupted, not wanting her to feel the tiniest sting of rejection. "'Cause I'm not sorry. I just think we're a little…off-kilter at the moment, and need to be careful." He reached out to brush a curl out of her eyes, startled by how temptation all surged back the minute he touched her. There was only a tiny thread of control keeping him from sweeping her into his arms again and soaking in that glorious energy she had. "Are you going to be okay?"

Melba leaned back against the door. "That's the big question, isn't it?" She hugged herself. "I don't really know."

"I think this is one of those things that don't work themselves out quickly. I'll pray for you." He surprised himself with that, especially now. How could he pray for a situation he was actively making worse? But how could he *not* pray? He wasn't a prayer-warrior kind of guy, but really, what else could be done in such a complicated mess? "I'm bad at prayer, but God hears even the bad ones, right?"

That pulled a thin laugh from her. "It can't get any worse, that's for sure."

Oh, Clark thought darkly, *I wouldn't be so sure about that.* "Call if you need me? No matter what time it is? I'm used to being interrupted, you already know that."

"My hero," she said with half a smile. She yawned, and he took that as a good sign. Clark allowed himself one small kiss on her cheek, memorizing the scent of her hair before pulling away to walk back into the darkness toward his car.

You should have told her, his conscience argued with him as he drove back down the narrow road. The irony of all of it struck him: she'd discovered she wasn't her father's daughter, but he'd discovered he was his father's son.

Chapter Sixteen

Melba placed the envelope on the table between her and her father. He'd seemed unusually lucid this morning, and she'd prayed for an hour before deciding it was time to talk about this. "Do you recognize this letter, Dad?"

"It's addressed to your mother." Melba couldn't tell if Dad's answer was evasive or just vague.

"It's a letter explaining who Danny Baker is." She felt it best to leave out the question of the author until she had a better idea of what Dad knew and what he was willing to admit. "That a man named Danny Baker is my biological father." Dad looked away, twisting the napkin at his place setting. "I know you know that, Dad. Can we please talk about it?"

Dad made no reply, nor did he meet her eyes.

"You're my dad. You'll always be the only dad I've ever known." At some point the previous night, she'd realized that that was true, and it felt good to say it. "But I need to sort this out and you're the only person who can help me with this," she continued. "I want you to help me with this."

After a long moment, Dad's face crumpled like the napkin. "I love you. You're mine." It was an angry declaration, daring the world to take away his little girl. It cut through her with such force it took Melba a moment to find her breath.

"I am," she said, grabbing his hand. "Nothing changes that, Dad. None of this changes that." The relief that it was finally out, that he was her ally instead of her obstacle in this, sent tears down her cheeks. "You're my dad." He shook her hand a bit, gripping tightly, as if to bind them to each other all over again. "I'm your Melbadoll, still, okay?"

"Okay." He blinked, a little confused, as if he was in the process of resetting his version of the world. "Now you know," he said quietly. "Now you know. Maria never wanted you to know."

"You tried to tell me that in the hospital. Did Mom make you promise not to tell me?"

Dad wiped his eyes. "Oh, what an argument that was. The only big one we ever had."

"Why didn't she want me to know…when I was old enough to understand? Surely she could see why I should know. In this day and age, it's not like…" Not like what? Melba really wanted to ask, "how could someone with Mom's faith act so deceptively?" but that wasn't a useful conversation right now.

"Your mom's father—your grandfather—wasn't a loving man. He was harsh and cold. She wanted you to live in a world where fathers adored their daughters, rather than abandoned them." Dad looked up at her, suddenly intense. "Your mother, you know how impulsive she was. The army sent word I'd been badly wounded, and she got scared. She was an emotional mess and she went to the wrong place looking for comfort. She made a mistake. The war was unpredictable—I was deployed so fast and no one knew for how long. We didn't have God in our lives back then, Melba. We were young. You can't hate her. She loved you so much. She wanted such a perfect world for you." He smiled. "She gave you those sheep, remember?"

The sheep were Mom's idea. Melba actually hated them at first, all clumsy and smelly. She'd asked for ponies or ducks.

"You asked your mama over and over to keep sheep. 'Like little Bo Peep,' you said."

He was drifting away from her. Melba squeezed her father's hand. "I wanted ponies. The sheep were Mom's idea, don't you remember?"

"She loved you so much. That was the worst, she used to say. She was okay with going home to heaven, but she hated leaving you. She wanted to live to see your wedding."

Melba hadn't even been in a relationship when Mom died. The cancer was spreading fast by the time she found out the truth; it wasn't like she had any chance of hanging on for some upcoming nuptials. Still, Dad's tone made it sound as though if only Mom could have just hung on a while longer... The way his mind twisted facts could be so cruel sometimes. "Dad." She squeezed his hand again, but his gaze was already far away and fuzzy. "Dad, who is 'G'?" She pointed to the return address on the envelope in a last-ditch effort to pull the facts from him. "Do you know who this letter is from?"

Her father ran his hand over the faded address as if his fingers might be able to feel the answer. Then his fingers fisted and he pushed the letter back over the table to her.

"Do we have any more cake left?"

If he knew, he wouldn't tell her. Worse yet, she couldn't even be sure he knew. More fighting with shadows. "Yeah, Dad," she said, feeling like her frustration would rise up and choke her. She swallowed it back. "Barney left some in the fridge. Cake would be nice."

Clark looked up when a shadow fell over the air compressor he was testing. He wiped the sweat out of his eyes to view Chad's stern face blocking out the slanted sun. Chad wasn't that much older than Clark, but there were days when it seemed like decades yawned between them. Today, as Clark sweated through his grey GFVFD T-shirt while Chad stood in a crisp white shirt and dark blue trousers, the difference felt huge.

"Take a walk," Chad said tightly.

Clark fumed. That was one of Chief Bradens's favorite euphemisms, GFVFD-speak for "I'm about to chew you out." Funny, Pop never bothered to take him into private when it was a family-related chastisement—he did those anywhere, anytime. "I'm not done here."

"It'll wait." That was decidedly not Chief Bradens that Chad was echoing this time. According to Pop, everything could wait until the equipment was correctly stowed—the next fire could be in ten minutes or ten hours.

"Okay," Clark said slowly, really not liking Chad's expression. He rolled the compressor to the side of the engine bay and narrowed his eyes at his friend. "But only because you still outrank me." That would be one of the more awkward pieces of Clark's ascent to chief;

technically, he'd outrank Chad and all their life it felt like Chad outranked him.

Chad settled onto the wrought-iron bench outside the firehouse, but Clark motioned for him to keep going. He had a pretty good idea what was coming and quite frankly, he wasn't sure he'd be able to keep it all in if Chad prodded too hard. When Chad hesitated, glancing at his watch, Clark shot him a look. "What? Do you need to be home for dinner?"

"I need to know what's going on." Chad's accompanying glare told Clark what he already knew; his temper had gotten the best of him this morning. Maybe it was better to get someone else's head in on this. Having lost his fiancée in a fire that he'd always viewed as preventable, Chad had closed himself off for years before Jeannie had cracked his heart open. Yes, he knew a thing or two about dark secrets and how they messed with a man.

"It's not a short conversation," he told Chad.

"I got time enough."

Clark led Chad all the way down to the riverbank and the footbridge over the Gordon River. Leaning heavily on the railing, Clark watched sticks and leaves float by on the current and fished for someplace to begin a conversation he didn't want to have.

Chad took the lead. "Jesse told me you were a mess out on the call this morning. That's not like you. Your father would tell you how you can't afford that right now."

"Oh, yeah, Pop would have lots to say about that." Clark didn't bother keeping the snarl out of his voice.

Chad leaned against the railing. "This is going to be hard enough without the two of you getting into it. George looks as bad as you today. Want to tell me what's going on?"

Clark let his head fall toward his hands. "It's a mess."

"What isn't?"

Clark grappled for a simple way to explain the knot of lies. Pop and Chad were close—he wasn't sure how much to reveal.

"Look—" Chad pushed back off the railing "—I'm not going to stand here and yank it out of you if you don't want to talk."

"Maybe you should," Clark surprised himself by firing back. "Somebody's got to help me make sense of this. Only it's…complicated. Private. Stuff that can't really get out, you know?"

Chad slumped against the railing again. "For crying out loud, Clark, what'd you do now?"

"Ha!" For the first time in forever, it wasn't about getting Clark out of some trouble he'd caused. That struck Clark as funny, and he let out a dark chuckle that made Chad raise one eyebrow. "Believe it or not, this one's not about my bad behavior."

"Delighted to know it. I think."

"Hold that thought." Clark turned to look straight into his friend's eyes. "I need your discretion in this. There are some dark secrets in all of it. I don't really want to involve you, but I could sure use your help to think it through."

Chad held his gaze, absorbing the seriousness in Clark's words. "Okay."

Slowly, Clark told the story. Parts of it came out in great, angry gushes, the hypocrisy of his father's words and actions boiling Clark's temper all over again. Other parts, like his powerful feelings for Melba and the secret of her parentage he wasn't sure it was even right to share, came out in slow, cautious words. "I hate telling you her secret," Clark admitted, "but it's so much a part of why this is crazy that I can't leave it out. It's all such a mess. Now is the worst possible time for all this."

Chad nodded, taking the whole situation in with the gravity it deserved. Chad was never one to spout platitudes or even be especially optimistic, although he had lightened up considerably since, as he put it, "God shoved Jeannie into my life." "It's so catastrophic I can't help thinking God is up to something huge. Neither you nor Melba knew any of this before yesterday?"

Clark shook his head. It felt oddly affirming to hear someone else call his current situation "catastrophic." For a guy who spent his days in continual crises, this one was pulling the rug out from under him in new and unnerving ways. "Melba said her father talked about it when he was out of it at the hospital. And you should have seen the way he roared at me." A new wrinkle occurred to Clark. "That means he must know. He must've thought I was Pop. They've never been cozy, Pop and Mort, and now I know why."

"Maybe not," Chad replied. "Just the rivalry for Maria could have been enough to keep them at odds. Mort may not know your dad did…what he did." Chad shook his head. "This doesn't sound like the George I know. Your dad is one of the most upstanding people I've ever met." Chad offered him a sideways glance of sympathy. "Even if he did ride you hard as a kid."

Clark pushed off the railing. "That's just it. He was always riding me about honor and character and all that. How could he stand there and do it, knowing he'd done something this underhanded?"

"People make mistakes. Huge things you can never take back." The shadow over Chad's face reminded Clark that his friend knew a bit about regret. "They change your focus forever."

Clark knew all this, but still couldn't stop the burning in his gut. "You're taking his side?"

"No, I'm not. I'm just trying to work out how the George I know could do what you've told me." After a pause, Chad added, "And what you need to do now with what you know. With what you feel."

"What I feel? I don't even know what I feel. I'm furious. My family feels like a sham—not as much as Melba's, but at least her parents *cared* about each other. About her." Clark leaned with his back against the railing, staring up as if the sky might drop a course of action down on him. "So now I'm supposed to add to her pile of pain by telling her my dad had a hand in all of this? Pop paid this guy to skip town on Maria. Offered to break up Melba's mom and dad's marriage even while he was my dad and married to my mom. What am I supposed to do with that?"

"They didn't, you know."

"Didn't what?"

"Maria and Mort stuck it out and made it work, and your dad stayed with you and your mom. Even you have to know he loved her…eventually. I'm not sure everyone gets the full-out fairy tale, you know?"

"Even you?" Clark had given Chad no end of teasing on how love-struck the guy had been.

Chad sighed. "You know Jeannie and I came into our relationship with a whole lot of baggage to unload. Whether or not we did it to ourselves, well, I'm not sure it matters. I do know that there aren't too many men who believe as strongly in grace as your dad. Maybe that's how he came to be the way he is, by slogging through all the damage he did."

"It's not okay," Clark blurted out. "I mean, I get what you're saying, but I'm not ready to call it all water under the bridge. I still want to punch the guy every time I see him." A thought struck him. "You know what I hate most? I hate that I finally meet someone like Melba and this whole load of damage comes flying up between us."

Chad smirked. "I know a bit how that feels. And that's really the issue, isn't it? What are you going to do about Melba?" His smile faded. "You know you have to tell her. There's a reason why you know the truth, and why you know now. She deserves to know, and I don't think you can count on your dad or hers to tell her."

"It'll ruin everything between us." Clark threw his hands in the air, frustrated. "And I don't even know what it *is* that's between us. I can't hurt her like that, not when she's still reeling from just knowing."

"You know that's not true. I think you know *exactly* what's going on between you and Melba and that has you terrified. Hey, it's the scariest thing there is to let someone in like that, and we're supposed to be the brave ones." Chad crossed his arms over his chest. "But think about one thing."

Clark sank back against the railing, the first wave of surrender hitting him, sucking out the sourness of anger and replacing it with the cool quiet of resignation. "What?"

"If you tell her, yes, there's a chance she'll take it out on you and it'll all go up in smoke. But if you don't tell her, then you'll never stand a real chance with Melba. It's the one thing your pop got right in all this—he demanded that all the hearts involved knew the truth. Even if it hurt. Melba has to know, and even a dumb lug like you can figure out God's placed you in the position to tell her."

He was right. The old Clark would have taken any easy way out of this mess, but he wasn't that man anymore. He'd come home to Gordon Falls for all the reasons he wasn't that man anymore. Clark let his head fall onto the forearms he rested on the railing. "When'd you get so smart?"

Chad fingered his wedding ring. "About the time I got so dumb as to fall for the candy lady." He leaned down on the railing so that his eyes were even with Clark's. "It's worth the risk. If you don't start with the truth, there's nothing to build on. I know, remember?"

"You're talking about Nick?" Clark asked. Chad nodded. He had been in the painful position of having to convince Jeannie that her son was in serious danger of becoming an arsonist. The poor kid was reeling from losing his home to a fire and it drove him into some dangerous behavior. God had placed Chad in the position of recognizing the truth Jeannie refused to see.

"I won't say it was fun, but we came through it stronger, closer to each other. If it's real between you and Melba, the same will happen to you." Chad's blue-green eyes bore into Clark. "Is it real between the two of you?"

Clark thought about the way he couldn't get her out of his head, the way her fragile strength cut through all his bravado, the way his soul seemed to settle beside her in a way he'd never known. "Yeah, it's real. Really, really real." He shivered. "God help me, I've no idea how to do this."

Chad let out a sympathetic laugh. "That's pretty

much how it works. You're at the top of my prayer list, Chief."

That was the term Chad reserved for Pop. He'd joked about not shifting it over until the day Clark was sworn in as head of the department. Evidently Clark had just earned his stripes. Either that, or it was Chad's tribute to a doomed man.

Chapter Seventeen

Melba couldn't have been happier when Clark called the next morning and asked if she had time to meet. Dad had two therapy sessions, so she had a good window of time—and they both needed it. After yesterday's failed conversation, her frustration made spending time with Dad more difficult than ever. "I'm getting to see why it's important I get a few breaks in my week," she said as they slipped into a booth at Karl's Koffee. "I'd go a little nuts myself if I spent all my time with him." She was unpleasantly surprised such mean and uncaring words could come out of her mouth, and she leaned back against the cushion and shut her eyes in remorse. "What an awful thing to say. Dad's not nuts. He's sick. He's…"

Clark reached a hand across the table. "Hey, don't beat yourself up. You're under a lot of strain. Even without all the…" his glance shot around the room and he lowered his voice "…complications, what you're doing is no small feat. I really admire you for coming back to him." That heartbreaker smile crept across Clark's face again. "I'm rather happy you came back to Gordon Falls right about now."

Clark laced his fingers with hers, something she'd cherished the other night on the steps. It was as if she could feel his strength seep into her when he did that. She tossed her gaze around the room as well, aware his hand was visibly linked with hers. "So you're okay with…this? We're not sticking to just being friends while you concentrate on your…" She stopped, unable to think of the word. "Exactly how do you become chief?"

"The ceremony involves a blood oath and a pound of flesh," he teased, his smile broadening when she laughed. Clark seemed to be the only person capable of making her laugh these days—even late-night phone calls to Charlotte didn't seem to brighten her spirits. "Actually, it was a town council vote—seeing as I'm a municipal employee and all. I'm already part of the department—the chief position takes effect at the end of the month. Barney tells me there's a party planned, but I figure that'll be more about celebrating Pop's retirement than about my promotion."

Something flashed through his eyes—something sharp and dark, like the opposite of a lightning strike. "You're good with that?" she asked carefully.

"Everyone can agree Pop's career is worth celebrating." There was something about how he said the words that let Melba know everything hadn't been smoothed out between father and son. "Not everyone is on board with my placement just yet. But you know," he said with a hint of defiance, "I don't think there's much I can do about that. I care about this town, I really do. Only people think what people think, no matter what. Most times they're wrong anyway so why bother?" His tone hinted at the old rebellious Clark, all long hair and black leather jackets.

"People will come around, you watch. The truth of your actions will show them, don't you think? You came back because Gordon Falls matters to you. You jumped in the river to get Dad out, you doubled back that first night to bring me dinner." Clark rolled his eyes, and she squeezed his hand. "You're a good guy, Clark Bradens, don't be so shocked by it." It struck her that for all his reformed behavior, Clark hadn't truly settled into his new life. Maybe that's why they were so good for each other. "You're a really good guy." She let her thumb run across the side of his hand, feeling the tendons flex at her touch.

To her surprise, he changed the subject. "How's your dad? Did you ask him about any of this?"

"Wow," Melba said, picking a chocolate chip off her scone.

"Wow, what?"

"I just realized that's the first time since I came here that I haven't started a conversation off with talking about Dad."

Clark took a gulp of his enormous coffee. "That's a good thing, right?" The guy drank the stuff like water. Perhaps all firefighters did, considering the hours they kept. He set down the hefty mug. "Did you get any answers?"

Melba pushed out a deep breath. "Some. Definitely not all." She looked up at Clark, surprised at the lump that rose in her throat even now. "He admitted it's true."

Clark's hand tightened on hers. "How was that? Hearing it from him?"

"Hard." She swallowed. "There's so much pain in his

face when he talks about it. I feel like I'm hurting him just by asking. Only I have to know. I have to know the truth, that's the only way I'll get through this." Melba broke off another bite of her scone, but her appetite had fled. "I hate this bit-by-bit unearthing, you know? Peeling off layers, getting one fact only to have new questions emerge. And really, now that his memories are getting distorted, how do I know what's fact at all?"

"Maybe you can't."

She frowned at him. It wasn't like Clark to offer such platitudes. "You know what the worst part is? I know it can't be true, but I feel like he somehow chooses to fade out on me when I ask something hard. As if he's choosing to hold things back, hiding behind the illness. I upended my life to come and help him with this, and he ducks out of the way when I ask him something that important? He owes me the truth! I get so mad." She pushed her hair out of her eyes, angry with herself. "And then I remember there's nothing to get mad at. Only there is, and I've got all this hurt boiling up inside with nowhere to go and…" Melba pushed back the plate holding the scone.

"Look, is it okay with you if we go somewhere with a little less of an audience? I'd offer you a boat ride, only that didn't go so well last time."

"Sure. I'd like that."

Clark stood and tossed a few bills on the table. She liked that he often overtipped. That had always been the sign of a good guy to her. "How about a walk?"

"A walk sounds great." Melba took the few minutes of steps down toward the riverbank to settle her spirit. She wanted to talk this out with Clark, but didn't want it to become an emotional escapade. Trouble was, she wasn't sure it was possible to avoid. At least a scene on the footbridge would be less public than one in the middle of Karl's Koffee. She loved the feel of him slipping his hand into hers as they walked. Clark had such a solidity of spirit. She felt like a walking cloud of vapors lately, without edges or any kind of backbone.

"I'm almost positive he knows more than he's telling me, Clark. It's like I can see the truth hiding in his eyes. I thought we were past this. And the clock is ticking, you know? I can't help but see time running out right in front of my face before he reaches the point where he truly won't be able to give me answers anymore. How can he think there's any point in keeping the rest of it from me? What's the point in hiding facts now?"

Instead of being empathetic, her little tirade seemed to bother Clark. He stiffened a bit, slid his hands from hers to grasp the bridge railing as they stared out at the current ambling along underneath them. "Maybe he's trying to keep from hurting you."

"It's not working. I'm one giant, walking ball of hurt. I think he owes me the truth. There, I said it. I want to demand it from him. I want to grab him by the shoulders and shake him and get him to understand how awful it is to know there are more secrets out there lurking." The tears started up, just as she knew they would. "I need to know that I know everything."

She expected him to take her and hold her, the way he did on the steps. He didn't. Instead, Clark looked at her and said, "You don't."

"I know I don't. That's the whole problem."

"No, you don't know everything because…because I haven't told you everything I know."

His admission slammed into her as if they'd opened

up the floodgates at the end of town. "What do you mean?"

"I know more than I've told you." He couldn't even look her in the eye when he said it. "I'm sorry."

Melba felt as if her last solid foothold had just evaporated. Truly, it was a falling sensation, just as surely as if she'd tumbled off the bridge into the river. "You're sorry? After everything I've told you, knowing how much I struggle with this, you kept a secret? What could make you do something like that? What do you know, Clark, what haven't you told me?" She wanted to take him by the shoulders and shake him. He was supposed to be the one thing she could count on in all this.

"I know who 'G' is. I knew it the minute I saw the letter."

Clark couldn't have picked a more damaging thing to say. She wanted to shout harsh, horrible words at him, but couldn't even pull in enough breath to make a sound.

Worse yet, Clark's own anger was rising up. "Don't you see, Melba? 'G' is George Bradens. My father wrote that letter. It's my dad who was in love with your mother. It's Pop who would have ditched his family—ditched me—if your mom was willing to run off with him. Can you see for a moment why that might be a bit hard to spit out?"

Melba's head was spinning. "How long have you known?"

"I recognized the handwriting. I went to him that afternoon and confronted him. He owned up to everything. Seems the upstanding fire chief wasn't exactly Father or Husband of the Year." Clark went to the other side of the bridge, staring at her with broiling eyes from the opposite railing.

"You knew when you came back to the house, and we sat on the steps? You knew *then* and you didn't tell me?"

"I knew I should but…"

"You coward!" The words lashed out of her, ripping her chest as they went. "You came to me. You let me sit there, knowing all my secrets and keeping yours, letting me kiss you, kissing me the way you did and…"

"Wait a minute, you were…"

"I was a wreck. I told you how much I needed to know the truth and you had part of it. Part you kept from me."

"I didn't know how to deal with it. It's terrible what Pop did. I hate it." He paced back over to her, and she sidestepped him. "It's even worse than you realize, Melba. Do you think I want to know what a sleazy thing my pop did? Do you think I'm happy to find out how far he would have gone—that he was willing to leave me and my mom for Maria? Do you want to know how bad it is? Do you want to know the whole, awful truth?"

Was he not listening to her? "Yes, I do."

Clark pulled both hands down his face, reining in his temper and lowering his voice. "My father paid Danny Baker off. He called in a few favors to get the guy transferred to some firehouse downstate and gave him a load of cash to disappear."

She couldn't have heard him right. "What?"

"You read the letter. Your mom came to my dad, desperate for a solution to a huge mistake of a one-night stand while your dad—Mort—was away in the Gulf."

"And *that's* how your father chose to help?"

"He thought that by solving this little complication, he'd get rid of his competition, and then win your mom over when Mort rejected her. Somehow the whole thing made a sick sort of noble sense to him at the time. He says he regrets it now, but who knows if I can believe anything? He didn't love my mom when he married her—the whole courtship story my mom told me growing up is a complete lie. My family is as messed up as yours, Melba, maybe even more."

"And you kept this from me?"

"It was a little hard to swallow, you know. At least your parents loved each other."

"That doesn't make this okay, Clark." She was starting to haul off at him again for his deception when the full extent of George's scheme hit her anew. "Wait— your father bought off my biological father? To win my mom?" Melba brought her hand to her forehead. The facts were whirling around her now, rushing together like some sort of awful television soap opera. "You knew this that first day and you kept it from me?"

"Not all of it. Look, you were a mess the other night. How was I supposed to heap this onto what you were already facing?"

"Oh, so you thought you'd protect fragile little old me. Maybe the apple doesn't fall too far from the tree. Your dad thought he was protecting my mom when he bought off my father."

Clark jabbed a finger at her. "That's not fair."

"Fair? You know what's not fair? I thought you were the one person around here I could count on and I was wrong, that's what's not fair." She turned and headed back over the bridge, wanting to put as much space between the awful Bradens men and herself as possible. How many more coffees—and kisses—would he have taken before he found it convenient to share what he knew?

"I'm sorry," he called, and she tried to ignore the pain in his voice. "This whole thing pulled the rug out from underneath me and I…" His voice caught and Melba stopped but didn't turn around. "I messed up. It's a gift of mine. Look." She could hear him coming close behind her. "I needed you and I was sure you'd push me away if I told you that my dad was the one who tried to pull your parents' marriage apart. I should have told you that night but you were so…so…"

His voice trailed off, and Melba remembered how she'd flung herself into his arms, an impulse to keep the pain at bay. They were so bad for each other right now, and yet so hopelessly tangled. There was nothing to do but walk away.

Which is what she did. Even when he called her name.

Clark let his head fall against the railing, feeling the anger and regret surge over him like the river current. He'd failed her. He'd made the wrong choice, had taken the coward's way out not once but twice, and now it had cost him Melba. The world felt as dark and forsaken as it had at the bottom of that fire so many years ago.

What's the point, Lord? Clark launched a silent howl at Heaven. *Why bring me home and pile on the pain? I've hurt everyone I care about, and people I care about have hurt me. This is why I came to Gordon Falls? This is what You had in mind? Why?*

"Why?" Clark yelled it out loud, listening to his anger echo across the riverbank. There seemed to be no point to any of it. No solution, only a frustrating maze of anger and mistakes. He looked back at the town and didn't see streets or buildings, but his history of mistakes and a future filled with nothing but more of them. What possible life could he build here now? The whole Gordon River didn't hold enough mercy to wash away all the damage he'd uncovered since his arrival. An ocean wouldn't hold enough. He couldn't see his way clear to forgiving his father, and that made him miserable. Mort and Pop would never forgive each other. Even the town wasn't ready to forgive him his own past.

Oh, but none of that even came close to Melba. He couldn't see how she would ever forgive him, and that seemed to suck his future dry. Clark wouldn't survive seeing that look in her eyes ever again, the aching accusation in them that told him how badly he'd let her down. He'd have to bear it every day in this tiny town. The weight of knowing he'd caused so much pain pressed against him until he didn't think he could breathe. She'd done something to him that could never be undone, pulled open a place in his heart that could never be filled by anyone else.

He stood on that bridge, stared at her car winding its way up the hill, and knew. Clark knew he was watching the love of his life leave his life forever. Only she wouldn't leave. She couldn't.

Which is why he had to do what he'd always been known for: walking away. Clark Bradens was about to live up to his reputation. Again.

Chapter Eighteen

Melba handed the knitting back to Jeannie. "See? You just knit that stitch when you should have purled. The rest is all right."

Jeannie eyed Melba. "Unlike you."

Melba sighed. It had been a whole day—a whole miserable day since her last talk with Clark—and she thought she'd kept her state better hidden than that. After all, this group wasn't exactly known for their ability to refrain from meddling. One slip, and she'd end up gushing out far more than was wise. That's why she hated secrets so much. All they did was throw walls up between people. Walls that could grow and expand years after the fact, as she was now learning. "No, I'm fine. Just tired. Dad got up a lot last night."

Jeannie resumed knitting but didn't look at the yarn. Instead, she bore into Melba with a mother's searing glare. "So your present state has nothing to do with why Clark Bradens is currently at the station trying to talk my husband into being fire chief instead of him? You have no idea why Clark might be fighting with his father and threatening to put a hundred miles between himself and Gordon Falls?"

"What?" Melba's knitting slid off her lap.

"I was waiting for you to bring it up," Abby said, "but honestly, if you sat there pouting one more minute I thought you were going to puddle into the couch cushions."

"Some of us go to Karl's Koffee, too," Violet said with a knowing smile, "not that you were noticing any other customers with that handsome man's hand holding yours."

"You're out of sorts and Clark is banging around the firehouse like an angry bull. It's not hard to connect the dots," Jeannie said.

"Give us some credit, dear, we were young once, too," Tina said. She came over and took Melba's hand in such a tender gesture that a small sob burst from Melba before she could hold it back. "Love is a very messy business indeed."

"Clark can't leave!" Melba blurted out. Then again, why not? What was keeping him here? Certainly not family loyalty—he clearly viewed any allegiance to his father as null and void now. And certainly not her.

"Well, I know that, and you know that, but someone had better tell that to the young man," Marge said. "You all must have had some whopper of a spat out there on the bridge."

Melba's eyes grew wide. "What did you hear?"

Jeannie dropped her knitting and put her arm around Melba. "Nothing, hon, but you can see that bridge from the windows at Karl's. It wasn't hard to guess the nature of the argu— conversation."

Tina squeezed Melba's hand. "Nearly two thirds of

the place was rooting for you to patch it up, if that makes you feel any better."

"Better odds than I expected," Marge interjected. "Seems that Bradens boy is finally growing on this town."

Angry as she was, Melba felt a pang of sympathy for Clark. Fully grown, about to take on a major managerial position, and people still referred to him as "that Bradens boy." *They're right,* she said to herself as she sank back into the couch cushions, *you can never go home again.*

"Do you want to talk about it?" Jeannie's gentle question was tempting.

"I can't, really." She dabbed her eyes with the Kleenex Tina pulled from the box on the parlor table. The gesture made her think of the many times—the *too* many times—Clark had handed her a tissue or handkerchief from his pocket. "It's complicated."

"When isn't it complicated?" Tina said. She let go of Melba's hand and touched her shoulder in such a motherish way that it made Melba's heart ache. "I know your mother's passed, but I think I speak for all of us when I say we'd gladly step in for you as that shoulder to cry on."

"That's really sweet," Melba said, feeling like God had handed her a whole handful of stand-in moms. It was a good feeling. "I'm just not sure there's a solution on this one."

"Nonsense," Violet declared. "God always has a solution, it's just that we can't always see it." She picked up her knitting and looked Melba straight in the eye. "Have you fallen for him?"

"You mean, like, in love?" Melba sniffed.

"No—" Violet thrust her knitting back into her lap "—I mean down his front steps—*of course* that's what I mean!"

"Violet," Jeannie chastised, "not everyone has your gift for…directness."

"*No one* has Vi's gift for directness," Marge muttered. Melba held in a snicker, for Marge could be oh-so direct herself. As if she'd heard the thought, Marge said, "But it would help us to know if you have."

"Help?" Melba moaned. "It makes it so much worse."

"Oh, there's where you're wrong," Violet countered. "Obviously, he's messed up, or you've messed up, or more likely both. Am I right?"

Melba started to launch into a condemnation of Clark's offenses, but Violet's question made her stop and think: had she hurt Clark? Didn't he find out something just as troubling about his family? "People in pain do stupid things," Melba found herself quoting Pastor Allen's most recent sermon.

Abby caught the reference right away. "Don't you hate it when God sends you just the sermon you need, often when you least want to hear it? What was the next part?" She held up a hand and wiggled her fingers as if to lure the memory in out of the air, finally snapping her fingers to say, "People of faith in pain do forgivable things, because people of faith are people of forgiveness."

"Doesn't get much truer than that." Marge nodded her head, then turned to Melba. "Did he hurt you, hon?"

"He did something that hurt me deeply." She couldn't go into any more detail than that, but Melba did surprise herself by adding, "But he did the wrong thing for the right reasons. I think."

"Was he sorry he'd hurt you?"

The sound of Clark calling her name, the forlorn repetition of it as it echoed off the riverbank…those things were wedged in her memory like thorns. He'd called her cell twice that day. She'd seen his car sitting at the end of her driveway late last night. She'd ignored him completely, some petty girlish part of her wanting the heartbreaker finally to get his due. "Very," she said, the single word her own condemnation. How many times had she snapped at people who couldn't seem to understand what having your life come unglued does to someone? She recalled the sharply worded memos about missed deadlines where she wanted to take a red marker and scrawl "My father is dying!" across the crisp black text. She'd wanted their understanding—but had she offered understanding in turn?

"I don't know what Clark did," Jeannie said, "but things can't be easy for him right now, either. It'd be a wonderful world if everyone behaved the way they ought to, but we don't. We mess up and hurt those we love most." Knowing what she knew of Jeannie, how she'd lost her husband, had her house burn, and been through a host of rough patches before finding love with Chad, the woman's words had the weight of hard-won truth to them.

Melba thought of her mother and father. How had they ever managed to piece their marriage back together after such a disastrous fall from grace? "It's all a big mess," Melba said, yearning to say more but knowing that wasn't possible.

"The world's a messy, broken, fallen place," Jeannie said, holding up her far-from-perfect knitting with a lopsided smile. Knitting wasn't coming easily to Jeannie, yet she still kept at it, taking out mistake after mistake until the new rows slowly built up. "But it's still a wonderful place. You said it the first day you came here. You said 'even bad knitting can keep you warm on a cold night.'"

Melba found the start of a smile. "I said that, didn't I?" It was one of her boss's favorite sayings.

"What if you and Clark are just hitting a patch of bad knitting? You don't want him to leave. I don't think he really wants to leave, or he'd have been gone already. What if you just have to take the time to undo the wrong stitches and keep going?"

"Maybe," Melba said, looking around the room.

Marge huffed. "I've had just about enough of these silly metaphors. Knitting, schmitting. Get out of here and go patch things up with that Bradens boy."

"That Bradens *boy*," Melba said, stuffing her knitting into her bag and finding her coat, "is a *good man*."

Clark refused to look at Chad as he stood in the back doorway of the firehouse. He'd hidden out here in the back courtyard, pretending to clean some valves, and wasn't in the mood for any more of Chad's lectures. Truth be told, Clark couldn't really say why he hadn't just thrown his things in the car and left already. If Chad had said he'd take on the job of chief, he would have. He wanted to.

Well, part of him wanted to. It was the other part of him that wouldn't let him just take off like he had all those other times.

"He's a hurt, angry guy who got stupid, Melba."

Clark stilled. She was here. *Lord, please don't let this hurt more.*

"Don't let him throw all this away," Chad was saying. "I know a thing or two about what a waste that is."

Clark didn't know if he could actually turn to look at her. He may have said Gordon Falls was his home, but it was Melba he couldn't really bring himself to leave.

"Hi." Her voice was small and shaky.

He turned to see dark circles cutting shadows under her eyes, and her hair looking like it had tumbled through a tornado. "Hi yourself."

She dropped her bag next to the door and twisted her fingers together. "Don't leave."

Her two words evaporated all the justifications he'd formed for why he ought to leave. He'd been sitting here cataloguing all the reasons why he really should put Gordon Falls in his rearview mirror, only to realize he'd just been waiting for those words. It would merely take that request from her to keep him here.

He told her the truth she deserved. "I don't know how to stay." She'd stolen his heart at her wit's end. At both their wits' ends, for he knew he had no way to pull either of them from this hole. He loved her, and hoped she loved him, but did that really fix anything? "We can't change all this mess. We can't make it go away or just decide it doesn't matter. It all runs too deep, you know?" He laid the brass fixture on the bench beside him. Ten seconds ago he'd vowed not to say this, but it came out anyway: "I can't be here and not be with you. I can't. Only I can't see how to stay and make this work, either."

"If you leave," she said softly, "all this will just follow you. I know. I thought about leaving, too. I mean, I know I can't—Dad and all—but I understand why you'd just want to walk away if you could. Only I don't think we're supposed to walk away from this. We're supposed to be here, you and me. We're supposed to get through this together." She sighed, her eyes glimmering with tears. "But, oh, this is going to be so hard."

Together. She hadn't ended it between them. His heart did a wild flip in his chest, pulling him up off the bench to take a startled step toward her. "You want to try? To see if we can do this?"

"I need to try, Clark. I don't think I can do this without you. It's going to take a whole lot of God and a whole lot of you to get me through what's ahead."

"Melba." Clark felt a wave of grace wash over him as he reached out to thread his fingers through hers. He knew, by the way his soul quieted at her touch, that he loved her. Chad was right; that made it worth the risk. "I am so sorry I kept anything from you. I told myself it was to spare you, but it was only me being a selfish coward." His other hand found a lock of her hair, curling it around a finger and watching what that did to her eyes. "You're so much braver than I am, did you know that? I spent a whole life running from problems, and here you turn and face them head-on."

Melba reached up and cupped his cheek, eyes crinkling in amusement at the scratch of his unshaven whiskers. He was a mess, had been since she'd walked away from him on the bridge. "Face them?" She shook her head. "It's more like I stand still long enough for them to swallow me whole. I was so busy wallowing in my pain I wouldn't see yours."

They both said "Forgive me," at the same time, and it was as if someone had lit a match in the dark. All the shadows fled in the face of one stubborn spark. Clark pulled her close, lost in the wonder of how she melted against him. *Oh, Lord,* he prayed, *thank You for her. Thank You for this.*

"Tell me how, Melba. Tell me what to do." He felt her cheek against his pounding heart, fought for breath as he buried his face in the top of her hair. Here he'd thought God had sent him to rescue her, when all along God knew they'd have to rescue each other. *You knew, You knew all along, didn't You?*

He felt her hands circle his waist, enjoying how right that was, reveling in what it felt like to look down into her eyes. The strangest expression came across her face.

"When you're knitting a very complicated pattern..."

"Knitting?" he rolled his eyes. "You pick *now* to talk about knitting?"

Melba laughed, a sound that doused him with happiness. "Stay with me on this one...it'll make sense."

Clark gave her a look of utter disbelief.

"As I said," she continued with that delightful determination of hers, "when you're knitting a very complicated pattern, you use something called a safety line."

"A safety line." He moved his face closer to hers. He was definitely not interested in discussing knitting technique at the moment. As a matter of fact, he had no interest in talking at all.

"No, really," she said, ducking her head against his advance and poking him in the ribs. She was going to have her say whether he wanted to hear it or not. There was something affirming in her clarity, as if the weight of the last days was slipping off both of them as they stood there. "This is actually important."

"I've got a whole other idea of important at the moment." His hand wound its way into her hair again.

"A safety line—" he watched her struggle to keep

her train of thought as his hand found the nape of her neck "—is a piece of different-colored yarn or string that you weave through a sound place in your work. The last good place you know where everything was okay. That way you can keep trying, but you'll be safe to undo the wrong stitches because they won't ruin the whole piece."

He had a pretty good idea of where this was going, and for once her crazy yarn talk made sense. "Where's our safety line?"

Melba moved to let her lips hover a fraction of an inch from his. "Right here. I love you." She offered him the tenderest of kisses.

And there it was. Clark encircled her, holding her as tight as he dared while he lifted her clear off the ground and kissed her back as if nothing else in the world mattered. Kissed her again as if all the pain the world could dish up would never overcome the power of those three words. "I love you, too." Clark murmured it into her hair, whispered into her ears, left it in a trail of tiny kisses down her cheek, poured it into his gaze as he stared at her twinkling eyes, and did just about everything else but shout it from the firehouse roof. "I am so unbelievably, breathtakingly glad that I love you."

Her sigh was a whole other sound from her earlier sigh—this one of bliss rather than stress. The whole silly safety-line thing made perfect sense. They were each other's anchor, each other's place to return to no matter how many times they stumbled in untangling the knots binding both their families. "I wish it solved everything," she said, laying her head on his shoulder.

"Maybe it only makes everything solvable. I suppose we'll just have to…" Clark cringed as his pager went off and the firehouse alarm split the air above them. Melba, who had clearly never been in the firehouse when the alarm went off, covered her ears and winced. "...figure it out later!" he yelled over noise and commotion. "I love you," he said into her ear as he turned to go.

"What?" she mouthed, cupping one ear. At least he thought that's what she said; it was getting harder to hear.

"I love you!" he yelled, determined to get that out at least one more time before he left.

Chad's bemused smirk as he ran into the engine bay told Clark he'd perhaps been louder than necessary.

Chapter Nineteen

Two weeks later, Clark stood on the firehouse roof and marveled at the May stars. It felt as if Heaven's grandeur had spread itself out before him to welcome him home.

"Chief." His father's voice came soft and hoarse behind him. Clark felt the weight of the word—it was the first time his father used the title. He was easing into his role, even comfortable with it, but from his father's lips the title was heavy and solemn.

"Chief," he replied. George Bradens would never stop being chief, even without the capital letter launching the word. It was who Pop was, always.

"I don't think I'll do this again," Pop said, rolling his aging shoulders. "Up on the roof is your deal, not mine. That stairway's too steep for my old knees." He pulled in a deep breath of the beautiful evening. "Pretty, though. I can see the attraction."

The sounds of the party spilled out from below them. He could hear Melba laughing with her friend Charlotte, who'd come out for the occasion and made some remark about a cousin who ought to come in as the department's first female firefighter. Pop had rolled his eyes, but Clark liked how he could consider the idea now that he was chief.

He was officially chief. Pop was "retired." It still stunned him to think of it. "They threw you a nice party, Pop. That's the nicest welcome party I never had."

Pop laughed. "It was supposed to be your welcome party, not my goodbye party. I hate parties."

"Which is why we threw you one without throwing you one."

"Those ladies ought to be ashamed of themselves. A lot of underhanded connivers, they are. The party was supposed to be for you."

Clark could only sigh. "I figured out a long time ago that it was never really for me." Pop started to protest, but Clark put his hand up. "I'm okay with it, actually."

"I'm not." Clark had known stepping down would be hard on his dad, but the whole day's events—the official handing over of the title and the party afterward—had beaten him down a bit. "Chief" was all Pop ever was, had been the focus of his life as long as Clark could remember. He was coming to realize the brave thing his father had done by stepping aside to let him take over. Clark was coming to realize a lot of things. Corny as it sounded, love had changed him deeply. So many misfitting parts of his life had slid into place under the grace of Melba's love. He understood grace and mercy in ways he never had—and probably couldn't have—before. Life was infinitely more complicated now, but better in more ways than he could hope to count.

He felt his father's hand grip his shoulder. While they'd managed a companionable speaking relationship, they hadn't touched since that angry night in Pop's kitchen. The touch weighed as heavily as the title.

"I'm…I'm sorry, son. For a lot of things. We didn't get most of it right, your mother and me, but you? You turned out…you turned out a better man than I."

The enormous lump in Clark's throat kept him from saying anything.

"You scared me to death most of your growing up and I think most of my hair is gone on account of you." Clark recognized Pop's humor for what it was— an attempt to cover the huge emotion of the moment. "But your mother would have been beaming today." He sniffed a bit and looked up at the stars. "I expect maybe she is."

"Yeah," Clark managed to choke out. "She'd be happy."

"She'd have hounded me until we patched things up." Pop stuffed his hands in his pockets. "I kept hearing her voice in the back of my head." He looked at Clark. "I did love her. We made it work. I don't think we would have if faith hadn't come into our lives a bit after…all that, but that's what God can do with a sorry situation like ours." Pop turned his gaze back out to the front of the firehouse, all strung up with little white lights for the party. "Your mother once said she thought maybe it was all in God's plan. Said she thought we might have never come to church if our marriage hadn't been so broken we were looking anywhere to fix it. Maybe so."

Clark thought about all the broken places he'd been, and the damage he'd done until he'd found himself lying in the bottom of that drainage well with nowhere to look but up. "Could be." He looked down at his father's truck, parked in the spot marked "Chief" for the last time. Someone had decorated the small sign for the occasion. He swallowed hard, knowing God had just handed him the opportunity to say what needed saying. "You know, Pop, I get it."

"Get what?"

"I'm not saying what you did was right, but I know you're sorry. And though I'm still messed up about how I'll handle it, I get it."

There was no need to talk about what "it" was—they both knew, had both carried the weight of it around for weeks. Pop didn't reply, but looked at Clark with a clarity the two hadn't shared in a long time.

"I'd do anything for her. I'd pay any price to be with Melba, to know my life would include her. I…" He wanted the right words to communicate the paradox of his thoughts, and they weren't coming. "It will be a long time before I'm at peace with what happened, but I do understand. What you felt. I don't think I could have until Melba. Until I felt the way I do." Clark held his father's eyes. "I'm done with all the hurt, I hope. I don't want us to lose the chance at these years ahead of us. You have my forgiveness."

They hugged, and Clark felt his father's breath catch with the emotion of the moment. "I needed that," Pop said, his voice rough and soft. "I'm so sorry."

They looked out over the town they both had sworn to protect. He really truly had come home. In so many more ways than he expected. Clark had always known he'd need a solid anchor inside to do this job. He'd looked for it when he bought the boat, but the true anchor was never out on the water. It was inside, in the tender space between himself and those he loved.

"I went to see him," Pop said quietly. "To put it right."

"Who?"

"Mort. Last week I met with Pastor Allen and talked

the whole thing out. He arranged for us to talk, to try to reconcile things. I thought I owed it to you and Melba if you were going to have any...kind of chance at... things."

Clark wasn't expecting that at all. Well, maybe in a couple of months—if they had that with Mort, for he seemed to be fading faster than anyone anticipated— but hardly now. "What happened?"

The pause before Pop answered was so long Clark began to worry. A long sigh filled the evening sky before his father answered. "He didn't recognize me. He didn't know who I was. So I just told him I was sorry but didn't have the heart to tell him why."

Sometimes, Clark thought, *grace isn't soft at all. Sometimes grace is so sharp it hurts.*

There was only one place to go. After she'd hugged Dad so hard he'd started scowling at her, Melba settled Dad in for supper with Barney and drove to Clark's house. She didn't even bother calling, didn't want to even try to go into this on the phone. This was face-to-face news. Her heart was an odd combination of pounding and peaceful as she rang his doorbell.

He was in jeans and a T-shirt, still toweling off his wet hair. "Hi there." The pleasure and affection in his eyes made her stomach do delightful flips. He'd been dashing in full uniform at the party two nights ago, but he was equally heart-stopping now, tousled as he was. "Just got in from a run."

I love him. It hummed through her with the same life-anchoring certainty of her earlier realization, the one she came to share. *I love him and he loves me.* It seemed too wonderful and yet effortlessly genuine—as if the world simply could not have lined up any other way. The whole day had sung that truth to her, hadn't it? Melba started to cry.

"Hey, whoa, everything okay?" Clark pulled her in and she soaked up the strength of his arms. He held her tight—assurance-tight but not smother-tight. Just perfect. It stunned her how a world so jumbled could settle itself into such peace even though not much had changed.

No, everything had changed. Everything that mattered.

"Melba? Love?"

The endearment only doubled her joy, and she looked up at him and tried to smile through the tears streaming down her face. "I'm fine. I'm wonderful."

His puzzled features told her he wasn't convinced. "You are? Want to explain?"

Melba held out her hand, knowing Clark would place a handkerchief from his pocket into her outstretched palm. "I'm not even sure I can. I want to try." She dabbed at her nose and eyes while Clark touched a tender kiss to the top of her head. "It's gone, Clark. *Poof,* gone in a wonder of a moment. I mean, I'm sure it's not completely gone, but just about."

Clark put her at arms' length. "You've lost me."

Melba shook her head. "Oh, I knew I wouldn't be able to explain this right." She let Clark pull her into his living room, settling her on his couch.

"Start over." His grin looked like he had all the time in the world, even though she'd just shown up on his doorstep unannounced. She smelled the soap on his skin as he wrapped an arm around her.

Breathing in a *Help me, God* prayer for some way to

put the last two hours into words, Melba reached into her memory for a sensible starting point.

Reach into her memory. She could do that. She could always reach into her memory. What a gift that was.

"Dad had a string of neurological tests done today—he gets them every month now—and Dr. Nichols asked to speak to me while Dad was busy with the technician. I thought he was going to ask me about Dad's little escapade yesterday with the coffeepot—I didn't tell you about that, did I?"

Clark raised an eyebrow. *Escapade* had become their code word for anything that went haywire in Dad's thought process and caused a commotion. Escapades were fast becoming a daily business. "We can skip over that detail if it's not important."

"It's not." Melba paused for a second to realize the genuine truth in her remark. She smiled. "It's not."

"So…" Clark cued.

"He didn't want to talk about Dad at all. He wanted to talk about me. He gave me a long, kind speech about the genetic path of Alzheimer's. He was very gently trying to tell me that I have a fifty percent chance of carrying the mutated gene that causes the disease. If the mutation is present, it's a hundred percent certain I'll get the disease. And I'd pass the same risk of mutation along to my children. He was so sweet about it, saying how hard this fact must be, how strong he thought I'd been through Dad's illness. He gave me the name of a genetics testing lab that could run a blood sample and tell me if I carried the mutation. He said he'd understand if I decided I didn't want to know, but that I could find out if I felt it was important."

Clark's face grew serious. "It *is* important, Melba. Have you decided if you want to know?"

Melba could only smile. Now she'd get to watch the same realization wash over Clark's face. "Clark, I *already* know. I don't have the mutation because Dad can't give it to me." It had taken her a second to put the facts together as well, and when she had, it had been enormously difficult to hide her emotions from Dr. Nichols. Hopefully the doctor took her shock to be from the seriousness of the decision, not the revelation that struck her.

Clark blinked, his eyes widening as he remembered what he knew. "He can't. He can't have passed the mutation on to you."

"Because while Mort Wingate is my dear dad, he's not my father." She grabbed at Clark's shoulders as tears fell anew. "God spared me. He spared my children. He gave me the best of everything even when I thought it was the worst of everything. I had the best father in the world but God protected me from the one thing Dad couldn't. It's a gift. It's a gift, not a mistake. All the hate, the anger, the blame, it all just dissolved the moment I realized it."

Clark shut his eyes for a moment, and Melba had the blessing of watching a deep gratitude come over his face. When he opened his eyes, they were full of emotion. "It never occurred to me, Melba. Not once."

"I know. I mean I should have put the facts together, but…"

"No," Clark said, taking her face in his hands. "I mean I would have married you anyway, even if you did carry the whatever-it-is. I'll stand by you no matter what."

"What?"

He blinked, truly unaware of what he'd just said. For a moment he just looked at her, and she saw the depth of his love in his eyes. The world unfolded a little further to hold all that new joy. Melba waited, her smile filling every inch of her heart.

And then it hit him, and he squinted his eyes shut and laughed. "I had it planned so much better than this."

Melba was not even trying to stop the tears streaking her cheeks. "Than what?"

"Out on the boat with a big ring and all kinds of romance. I had the storybook proposal all planned. And now I've sort of botched it all to pieces, haven't I? Another Clark Bradens mess-up."

"No, it's perfect. It's all perfect. Messy, but perfect, so it fits right in."

He kissed her. "Nah, I can't do it like this. It's got to be done right." He pulled back a bit, and she recognized the look of a plan brewing in his eyes. "Give me back my handkerchief."

"Huh? It's already wet."

"That won't matter. In fact, I think it kind of adds to the whole thing. Close your eyes."

Stumped, she followed his instructions, laughing at the humming he made while he did whatever he was doing.

"Okay."

Melba opened her eyes to see Clark's breathtaking smile above the white square he held. Scrawled in ballpoint ink—she didn't know where the pen came from and she didn't care—was "IOU 1BIG?"

"I owe you one big?"

Clark rolled his eyes. "One big question, *the* big question. Done right. All the trimmings."

"But I'd say yes right now and...?" He didn't let her finish the thought, silencing her instead with a kiss that made the world reel around her.

"Because," he said when they paused to catch their breath, "we're home here and we've got all the time in the world."

* * * * *

Dear Reader,

Life has a way of tangling us up. Mistakes heap pain, illness robs the innocent, disasters happen, and a broken world threatens to pull down our faith. Hard as it can be, our finest defense is always grace. In my world, grace often comes in knitted form. Years ago, I began a prayer shawl ministry at our church on the recommendation of a fellow knitter. It's been one of the most amazing, rewarding, faith-building experiences of my life. If you'd like to know more about how to implement a prayer shawl ministry in your community, get in touch with me at www.alliepleiter.com or P.O. Box 7026 Villa Park, IL 60181, and I'll be happy to share information and encouragement.

Questions for Discussion

1. Has someone ever given you a helping hand during a crisis? How did it bolster your ability to cope?

2. Was there a Clark Bradens in your high school? What did people think of a shady character like that? Do you know what happened to him?

3. Charlotte says Melba "needs backup." When was the last time you called in friends to help you in a tight spot? When did you fail to reach out?

4. Clark says "you never get hurt running to something, you get hurt running from something." Do you agree? Why?

5. Does your church have "a deacons' board like a SWAT team?" Is that ever a bad thing?

6. Have you had a secret pull the rug out from under you? Do you feel you handled it well? What would you change if you had the opportunity?

7. What's your opinion of Clark's "Escape Clause" tactic? What do you do to keep an even keel when life gets hectic?

8. Mort seems to have given many people in Gordon Falls their first job. What was your first job? What did you learn about life from it?

9. Have you ever longed to ask your parents what their marriage was like before you were born? Why or why not?

10. Were Clark and Melba right or wrong to switch off their cell phones—even for thirty minutes?

11. What would you do if you found a stack of old letters between your parents?

12. George says "The world is full of things we all regret and can't fix. It's the whole point of grace." Where has this been true in your life?

13. Melba draws much comfort from Psalm 139. Is there a psalm that has stood out like that for you in your life?

14. Melba tells Clark, "If you leave, all this will just follow you." Have you experienced that in your own life? What did you take away from that experience?

15. What—or who—is your "safety line"? If you don't feel like you have one, what can you do about it?

REQUEST YOUR FREE BOOKS!

2 FREE INSPIRATIONAL NOVELS
PLUS 2
FREE
MYSTERY GIFTS

Love Inspired®

The pavement outside the Kansas City airport radiated heat
even though the sun had already sunk below the horizon.
Tate held his seven-year-old daughter's hand a little tighter
and squinted against the dying sunshine to read the signs
hanging overhead.

"That's it down there," he said, pointing. "Baggage
Claim A."

Lily Farnsworth was the last of six new business owners
to arrive, each selected by the Save Our Street Committee of
the town of Bygones. As a member of the committee, Tate
had been asked to meet her at the airport in Kansas City and
transport her to Bygones. With the grand opening just a week
away, most of the shop owners had been at work preparing
their stores for some time already, but Ms. Farnsworth
had delayed until after her sister's wedding, assuring the
committee that a florist's shop required less preparation than
some retail businesses. Tate hoped she was right.

He still wasn't convinced that this scheme, financed by a
mysterious, anonymous donor, would work, but if something
didn't revive the financial fortunes of Bygones—and soon—
their small town would become just another ghost town on the
north central plains.

Isabella stopped before the automatic doors and waited

for him to catch up. They entered the cool building together. A pair of gleaming luggage carousels occupied the open space, both vacant. A few people milled about. Among them was a tall, pretty woman with long blond hair and round tortoiseshell glasses. She was perched atop a veritable mountain of luggage. She wore black ballet slippers and white knit leggings beneath a gossamery blue dress with fluttery sleeves and hems. Her very long hair was parted in the middle and waved about her face and shoulders. He felt the insane urge to look more closely behind the lenses of her glasses, but of course he would not.

He turned away, the better to resist the urge to stare, and scanned the building for anyone who might be his florist.

One by one, the possibilities faded away. Finally Isabella gave him that look that said, "Dad, you're being a goof again." She slipped her little hand into his, and he sighed inwardly. Turning, he walked the few yards to the luggage mountain and swept off his straw cowboy hat.

"Are you Lily Farnsworth?"

*To find out if Bygones can turn itself around,
pick up LOVE IN BLOOM
wherever Love Inspired books are sold.*

SADDLE UP AND READ 'EM!

This summer, get your fix of Western reads and pick up a cowboy from the INSPIRATIONAL category in July!

THE OUTLAW'S REDEMPTION
by Renee Ryan
from Love Inspired Historical

MONTANA WRANGLER
by Charlotte Carter
from Love Inspired

Look for these great Western reads AND MORE,
available wherever books are sold or visit
www.Harlequin.com/Westerns